LOVING DANGEROUSLY . . .

"You ever been initiated into the Mile High Club?" Scott asked as we pulled into the airport. We were heading toward a bright yellow Cessna.

"Mile High Club?"

"Great initiation," he said, stepping agilely onto the wing.

I followed him, less agilely, into the cockpit. "But who flies the plane while we . . ."

"Automatic Pilot."

"How nice of him." I laughed nervously, surveying the complex instrument panel.

"Are you scared?"

"No."

"Good, then let's get this mother up and put the fear of God in you. . . ."

6 DAYS, 5 NITES

Susana de Lyonne

FAWCETT GOLD MEDAL • NEW YORK

6 DAYS, 5 NITES

Published by Fawcett Gold Medal Books, a unit of CBS Publications, the Consumer Publishing Division of CBS Inc.

ISBN 0-449-14028-8

Printed in the United States of America

10 9 8 7 6 5 4 3 2 1

6 DAYS,
5 NITES

1

I had my first urge to travel when I was two, but my trip was cut short by a concerned policeman who returned me home after I'd only gone five blocks. I couldn't understand my mother's panic. It had been an exhilarating adventure.

By the time I was twelve, I was scanning tour brochures and marking up road atlases with impossible itineraries. When some cousins moved to Honolulu and invited me for the summer, I leaped at the chance and braved the pre-jet-days, nine-and-a-half-hour flight by myself. I learned to surf, paddle an outrigger, gyrate my hips in a shocking Tahitian dance, and I had my first real kiss under the heady fragrance of wild ginger blossoms, in lush green mountains behind the sugarcane fields. My first contact with the exotic, and I was determined to have more.

By the end of my sophomore year in college, I had been across the United States, through Western Europe, and had nearly failed a summer session at the University of Mexico because I spent too much time in Acapulco.

And still, I might add, miraculously maintained my virginity. It was, however, ready to pop.

This brings me to the immediate cause of my becoming a professional travel agent and not just another wanderlusting young woman. It was the summer of '65, Lake Tahoe, California. I've never been a girl men turn around to gape at—except in the summer when a dark golden tan sets off my blond hair, and I'm wearing nothing but a bikini. The fine arts of cosmetology and fashion coordination elude me. I've often thought if I could breeze through life naked, with a sun lamp, I'd be an eternal knockout.

A mustard-smothered hot dog in hand, I was crossing King's Beach in front of some raucous, beer-drinking, fraternity men who were trying desperately to get my attention. One of them stuck his foot out and tripped me. Perhaps I should have taken it as an omen, but all I saw, looking up from the sand, was Al's huge, warm smile. A smile that seemed to engulf the whole world.

The Free Speech Movement at Berkeley was making headlines that fall, but I found it about as scintillating as a morning fuck on a hangover. I was madly, breathlessly in love with Mario Savio's antithesis: A Frat Man. My parents were thrilled I'd finally brought home a clean-cut, decent, All-American Boy. They had been polite, but never terribly pleased about the handsome ("too handsome," my mother claimed) bullfighter who had followed me home from Mexico City the summer before. But Al charmed my parents, my aunts and uncles, my dog and cat. He could charm anyone. We were a cozy couple, content on a Saturday night to sit by the fire and sing folk songs, rather than party. Under the glib, smiling exterior I found a serious, introspective, young man. We talked earnestly about traveling together to Iberia, and, finally, about marriage. I even found myself in unguarded moments picturing him as the man I wanted to father my children.

The night we were pinned, my sorority sisters stood on the porch with candles, singing the pinning song to Al's fraternity. No Sound and Light Festival at a Loire Valley chateau could have been more spectacular to me at that moment. The same night, in the Berkeley Hills, overlooking the lights of San Francisco, in the back of his VW, I gave Al my precious cherry. We watched the sun rise over the bay, as we sang Kingston Trio songs to his guitar. I taught him the words to "Tom Dooley" in Spanish.

Trouble started, as close as I can pinpoint, when Al changed his major from business administration to history in an effort to find himself and the meaning of life. It wasn't long before he dropped out of the fraternity and into a dirty apartment off Telegraph Avenue. Frayed jeans, beard, marijuana —all followed in rapid succession.

The final blow fell when he gave up the Kingston Trio to embrace Bob Dylan. Once Al hooked up the harmonica to his guitar, he ceased to need me for harmony.

Our sex life had dwindled into:

"Sorry, Emily, it must be the uppers. Or maybe it was the downers."

"Maybe it was the LSD."

"No, LSD wouldn't do that."

"Well, don't worry about it."

"But a man's never supposed to lose his individuality or his masculinity."

"Al, let's go to sleep. I'm sure you'll regain them in the morning."

I waited patiently for morning. *As soon as he finds himself,* I thought, *he'll realize how much he loves me and we'll fly off to Spain for our honeymoon.*

But there were nights I arrived at his apartment when he didn't recognize me—and then came the morning I couldn't wake him. His car engine had been disassembled neatly on a bedspread on the living room floor in a semicircle around him. The strings of his smashed guitar had been threaded through the pages of a term paper I was writing for him on the effects of the Industrial Revolution in Europe.

I stayed at the hospital two days waiting for him to come out of the drug-induced coma. It occurred to me that he may have lost his mind entirely. I was frightened, but knew I had to stay with him. After all, I loved him. That meant for better or for worse, didn't it?

The first week out of the hospital Al shaved off his beard, washed his jeans, and even got it up twice in one night. I was delirious with joy. Until I became vaguely aware of the feeling my sorority sisters used to call "Nausea-Cock-in-the-Throat." I told Al what I suspected. He went out and bought a lid of grass.

A doctor confirmed it; I was pregnant. Al was stoned when I called to tell him. "Are you sure it's mine?" was his indifferent response.

"No!" I shouted, "I must have sat in something!" Looking back on it, I realized that very few of the college men we knew coughed up money or even moral support for our abortions. Even fewer made good on their marriage proposals. Al never called me again.

I took the necessary five hundred dollars from my savings account, and because it was 1966, went to Tijuana. At the prearranged meeting place I got into a black Chevy with four strange girls. A burly man named Chucho took our cash and drove us silently out of town. We were too terrified to talk to each other.

A motel room doubled as an operating room. We went in one at a time. I was first. My legs were shaking as I placed my feet in the stirrups. Knees fell together protectively. The doctor—I hoped he was a doctor—smiled.

A white sheet covered my legs. I couldn't see. There was a warm instrument thrust into me. Would they put me out? Would they please tell me? Something? Anything? The instrument thrust in and out. A familiar rhythm. Warm, like a man's body. The doctor smiled.

I opened my mouth to scream.

A needle went into my arm. When I awoke with the four strange girls in the motel room, I knew the fetus had been scraped from my uterus. Al's unborn child lay bleeding on the cutting-room floor of a sleazy Mexican motel.

My honeymoon castle in Spain? One of the girls was weeping quietly. Another mumbled incoherently in her sleep.

I was angry.

How could I have been so stupid? To be duped into believing in Love, in Happily Ever Afters. Prince Charming had callously machine-gunned me down when my back was turned. Well, I just wouldn't turn my back again. The next man, I vowed, I'd grab by the balls, and I'd run things my way.

How clear it all seemed projected up on that cracked motel room ceiling. The gnawing frustrations of the past few months were at an end. I knew exactly what I wanted to do with my life.

2

"I'm quitting school," I announced to my bewildered parents a few nights later.

"But, Emily, what are you going to do?"

"I'm going to be a travel agent." I might have said "snake-charmer," the way they stared at me.

"Why a travel agent?" asked mother.

"I like to travel. I think it would be fun."

"Life isn't all fun, you know," she replied, looking very motherly. "It's time you learned that." She looked to my father for confirmation. He nodded, but I could tell he wasn't in the mood to be parental.

"Once you get your teaching credentials," she continued, "you can play around with—"

"I don't want to be a teacher. I don't even like children."

"You don't have to like them to teach them. What about teaching high school or even college?"

"I'm sick to death of the academic world! I've been in nothing but school since I was five years old!"

"Actually, we enrolled you in nursery school when you were three. A child psychologist told us you were difficult, because you needed to be around children your own age." She loved to repeat the story about how impossible I was to control, because I was an only child. When I was angry, I would take all the toys out of my little red toy chest and smash them against the walls or against anyone who happened to be standing nearby. I was famous for my swift kicks and sharp teeth. The nursery-school teacher finally cured me by kicking and biting me back, something my parents and the child psychologist never had the nerve to do.

Eventually, I dropped much of this antisocial behavior. I learned there were more effective, less violent methods of getting your own way.

This evening was an exercise in that. Since I had spent my entire savings account on the abortion, my new plans depended on some financial assistance from home. Disapproval in my family always was accompanied by the withholding of funds. I had yet to learn how easy it was to earn my own living.

"Tell me," demanded my mother. I could tell by her expression that she was about to reason with me. "How do you expect to earn a living at this—this travel business? What do they make, Joe?"

He shrugged his shoulders. "A couple hundred a month? I don't know." He was in auto parts. Once a year he and Mother took a cabin up at Lake Tahoe. I don't think they'd ever even been to a travel agent.

"A couple hundred a month barely covers your wardrobe, Emily!" expounded Mother.

"Well, there are a lot of benefits," I argued.

"Medical? Dental? Retirement?"

"I'm not sure about that, but I know you get discount airline tickets, free hotel rooms, and—"

"And only two weeks a year vacation to travel in, and no money to spend once you get there," added my father. Money matters were clearly his field. The conversation had finally begun to interest him.

"It's Al, isn't it?" said my mother suddenly. "You don't want to go back to school because of him." My mother was never far from the truth, though I'd never admit it. "They broke up, you know," she informed my father, to whom all my boyfriends, except the bullfighter, looked alike. "How about transferring to UCLA or Santa Barbara? Although Santa Barbara doesn't have much in the way of graduate schools."

"Graduate school! I don't even want to finish college," I reminded her, though I knew exactly what she meant.

"Well, just whom do you think you're going to meet in a dinky travel agency?" she mustered with the full force of her fifty experienced years.

I shrugged my shoulders indifferently. Romance was understandably ranking very low on my priority list. Parental approval, due to my lack of funds after the abortion, ranked very high. My mother was a lost cause, I decided. However, she didn't control the purse strings. I would have to direct an appeal to my father.

"Look," I said, trying to sound as reasonable and adult as possible, "I know an education is important. Probably after six months, I'll decide to go back to school. Right now I want to strike out on my own. I want to know what it's like to have a job and work for a living. I want the responsibility of being" (and this was aimed directly at my father) "completely self-supporting."

The arrow hit its mark. "I think we ought to let her give it a chance," he said. "It's not like she's dropping out to become a vagrant beatnik. She wants to do something constructive." My mother had lost too much ground to rally another offensive. She sighed, lit a cigarette and watched her dreams, of my marriage to some enterprising young law student, go up in smoke.

"We've got some contacts in the travel business," added my father as he shook out the evening paper in front of him. "Remind me. I'll give them a call in the morning."

3

It was a foggy, cold San Francisco morning in the middle of June. Neatly attired in a three-piece navy blue knit suit and white gloves, I boarded a bus not far from my parent's Sea Cliff home. It was my first job interview: one of my father's contacts.

All around me, people hurrying to work, popping out of little Victorian houses, reading the *Chronicle*. I was part of them for the first time. It sent tingles of adult responsibility down my spine.

I was about to take on the magnificent Matson Lines. I imagined myself a social director, elegant, charming and bubbly on the *Lurline,* sipping champagne with a captain who looked like Cary Grant.

My interviewer looked more like Don Knotts. A friend told me the trick in an interview with a man is to look at him like you want to give him a blow job. I glanced down discreetly, but saw no evidence of his masculinity. Perhaps it had been shot off in the war. I tried to think of something else to give him.

"Do you have a resumé?" he asked, suppressing a yawn. Three years of college and a lot of traveling hadn't produced any actual job experience, I explained.

"How fast do you type?"

17

"Seventy words a minute." His eyebrows raised slightly over his horn-rimmed glasses, as if to say, "You're probably full of shit." Instead, he reached into his drawer and produced a typing test.

So you don't believe me, Mr. Cockless. Wait 'til you see what a hot-shit typist I am. I was the star of my high-school class. He led me to an empty desk in a large room adjacent to his glass-enclosed cubicle. Fluorescent lights glared down on me from above, while fifty women at fifty beige metal desks tapped noisily away all around me. I slipped the white paper into the IBM, arranged the test at an angle to my right. Cockless punched the stopwatch. Off I went.

Nimble fingers flew over the keys. I'd show him how fast and accurate a college dropout could be.

"No shorthand?" he yawned, scanning my perfect typing test.

"No."

He shook his head sadly. "Your typing is excellent, Miss Davis. We could place you in the typing pool if you'd agree to take a night course in shorthand. In a year or so you could move up to junior steno. If you're good," and he paused here to give it emphasis, "maybe eventually, an executive secretary."

I suddenly saw his little beige cock rising like a sail above the metal desks of the typing pool. A person could drown in a typing pool.

Contacts, I thought grimly, leaving the Matson Lines. I could probably find as good a job on my own. I picked up a *Chronicle* and stopped for a cup of coffee that warmed my frozen nose and

fingers. My feet were already hurting from the
unaccustomed high-heeled shoes; the panty girdle
was cutting off circulation to my brain.

There was one ad for a travel agent. "Experience
mandatory," it read. I flipped in desperation to
Herb Caen. Perhaps he could cheer me up. The
whole article was a jibe at Los Angeles—something
about it being a smile in search of a personality.
Native San Franciscans are acutely aware of our
superiority to the Southlander. We have culture,
traditions, history.

History. I was sick of history. That's what had
mucked up Al. If he'd only stuck to business
administration—

If I had to start at the bottom of some company
somewhere, why not make a complete break with
my own past?

My parents greeted this new inspiration with
even less enthusiasm than they had my last. The
only saving grace, according to my mother, was
that I'd arranged to stay with my cousin Cindy.
"Cindy just might be a good influence on you,"
said my mother wistfully, as I boarded the PSA
flight to Los Angeles—a personality in search of a
smile.

4

Cindy was the success story of the family, her mother, the failure. My aunt Rita had been so beautiful that many, many, many men wanted to marry her. Consequently, she picked the one bad apple in the barrel. I never understood what great beauty had to do with making a bad choice. I'm just repeating the story as it was told to all the little-girl cousins in a very large family. Aunt Rita was always the Divorced Aunt, who lived, we assumed, unhappily off a meager alimony in Los Angeles, where divorce wasn't such a stigma.

Cindy, everyone said, was almost as beautiful as her mother had been. But Cindy had the important ingredient her mother lacked: style. I knew much of her wardrobe was inexpensive and hand-made, but Cindy made it look like Givenchy designed it for her. She brought to the drab, gray Berkeley campus an essence of Hollywood glamour. Her first semester she was sweetheart and queen of everything.

I might have been insanely jealous, our being so close in age, but I really liked her. The year I entered Cal, she was a senior and still living in the sorority. I never wanted to join. Being crammed into a house with sixty coeds who were studying frantically to be second-grade teachers appealed to

21

me as much as joining a convent. But those were the years parents still felt an impressionable young lady needed moral guidance and rules to follow. It was either join the sorority or commute from home. I became increasingly dependent on Cindy to make sorority life bearable.

Among other oddities of secret, most sacred rites, there existed a point system that required each new member to do a number of "good deeds" for the older girls. You could not be initiated without at least a hundred points. I have never been one to kiss anyone's ass. I figured the eighty-dollar initiation fee my parents plunked down entitled me to be a member. A week before initiation, Cindy was informed that her cousin would not be allowed to join unless she made up the points like the other girls.

Cindy called me to her room and shut the door. From under her bed she pulled out a bottle of vin rosé and another of Seven-Up. "You know how to make a wine cooler?" she asked me. Liquor was strictly forbidden in the house. I shook my head. She explained the method and added, "For every wine cooler you make us, I'm going to give you twenty points."

That became the memorable night we took the solemn sorority song that began:

As sisters all we stand
All over this great land. . . .

and transformed it into the enduring classic:

As sisters all we fuck
Whenever we're in luck. . . .

Cindy's sage advice to me about the sorority on her graduation day was, "Don't take any bullshit from these assholes. They need you more than you need them." It was sound advice. I may have not been Sweetheart of Sigma Chi material, but I did have that all-important attribute that kept the good-looking fraternity men buzzing about "that cute blond pledge." Cute blondes gave a sorority status, and they would forgive you your transgressions as long as you kept them relatively discreet.

Everyone was surprised when Cindy didn't make off with a husband before getting her degree in psychology. Obviously she was not going to make a hasty decision, as her mother had done. Instead, she took a job in the personnel department of a large insurance company. She was bright, worked hard, and in a year was in complete charge of clerical hiring.

For Cindy, personnel work was a logical career. At her fingertips was the vital information— marital status, income, and background—of any man in the company who asked her for a date. "Even more important," she added, "I got first crack at the new arrivals."

Bob Daniels had barely been in town from Chicago a month when Cindy was marching down the aisle with him. Everyone agreed that she'd made a superb choice. Well-dressed, well-educated, full of drive and ambition—at forty, he was one of the company's top executives and climbing fast. I thought he looked a little pasty and balding, but my mother assured me that good looks weren't all that desirable in a husband. "Looks fade, you know." Her reference was to Aunt Rita's ex-husband who was only a bloated vision of his former self as he guided Cindy down the aisle to the arms of her new mate.

Husband Bob was out of town when I arrived in LA. We drove up the circular driveway to their newly acquired Bel Air villa, in Cindy's powder-blue Mercedes with matching upholstery. It was a large, Spanish-type home with rolling lawns, geraniums, maple trees, graceful archways and enclosed tiled patios. I was entranced.

"You don't know how dull Bel Air can be," confided Cindy to me during the second cocktail of the afternoon as we sat by her pool. "People who live around here really aren't my age. Friends I had from high school or college are still struggling in apartments. Of course, when Bob's here, we get out and do things. But he travels a lot with his job."

I disliked little Bobby immediately. Like those of most small children, his demands for attention taxed my already-thin patience. When I tried to ignore him the day I arrived, he grabbed the end of my tit in his little fist and made an excrutiating 360-degree twist. Cindy and her Mexican maid were always quick to respond to his every whim. He had them trained.

Cindy's personnel background was a great help in finding me a job. She knew all the good employment agencies, which, in turn, sent me on some excellent job interviews. Unfortunately, no travel agency wanted to take the time to train a new employee. Rate structures and ticketing were too complicated for a novice.

I settled for the next best thing, an Argentinian export company which sold some Central American airlines tickets under the table. Cindy thought I was crazy for taking a job at $350 a month, but they promised to teach me "ticketing," and I needed that experience more than money.

The airline sales representative, Ed Rodriguez, proved to be an excellent teacher. I wasn't sure if his motives were to get me to sell more tickets or to get me to bed. His gallant efforts did not go unrewarded in one sense. I sold a lot of tickets.

Ticketing, I discovered, is an intricate, mystical procedure that airlines have evolved to slow down the sale of their precious commodity and confuse travel agents. If a passenger, for example, wants to fly to Chicago and back, one cannot simply add together two one-way tickets. A five-inch-thick Rate Book, filled with electrical-circuit-looking diagrams, suggested a number of interesting ways to arrive at a fare. A round-trip ticket offered the first discount to your delighted passenger. If he was a member of a family, he might be eligible for a family-plan discount. Flying on certain days of the week he could get an excursion-fare discount. If he didn't mind flying late at night, he could qualify for lower fare.

Things got even stickier with stopovers. Excursion fares weren't allowed if the client made more than one. If he was going to make a number of stops, you had best consult a diagram and determine your maximum mileage. Domestic rules were often not the same as international rules.

Finding your poor passenger's flight to Chicago was also made difficult. The schedule book for domestic flights was as thick as a telephone directory. All the vital information was in code—from cities to flight classes. Cities like New York had three airports. There was a separate code for each. Another clever code would tell you which flights were nonstop and which made five stops. This was crucial, I learned after booking one irate customer on a three-stop night flight to New York.

Finally, all this information had to be transferred onto an airline ticket, a finger-breaking exercise to press through up to six carbon copies. Again, all the ticket information was in code, including how you managed to arrive at a fare. If you made a mistake, a ticket agent at the airline ticket gate might stop your customer and ask him to pay the difference.

Ed taught me many shortcuts to the procedure. The most useful of these was his advice to call the airline ticket offices when in doubt. Most airlines employed special people just to deal with travel agents. Once you learned the codes, it was like conversing in a foreign language. Your customer didn't have to be aware of how little you really knew.

After I'd been at the export company a month, Ed Rodriguez told me about the job opening at Royal Beverly.

"Do you think I have enough ticketing experience?" I asked him.

"Honey," he laughed, "you've got brains. The ticketing you can fake."

5

I arrived nervously at the sleek, glass and concrete high-rise on Wilshire Boulevard. Royal Beverly Tours and Travel was on the fifth floor. A starlet receptionist greeted me with a polished Ultra Brite smile, pushed the intercom with a carefully manicured fingernail, and announced my arrival to the general manager, Mr. Garrison.

I glanced around the small reception room. Aside from the receptionist, there was nothing decorative in it. An old Hawaii travel poster, featuring a blond, tanned surfer, and a rack of tour brochures, were the only indications this was not an insurance agency. I sat down on an uncomfortable green plastic chair and began filling out the form application.

The office door opened and a tall, stunning, olive-skinned redhead emerged. My first impression of Nicole was that she was an extraordinarily beautiful young woman. It was a while before I realized her features were quite plain, and that she was well into her late thirties. There was no painted illusion of Hollywood face-lifting makeup to Nicole. Her secret: she was firmly convinced of her beauty, and, being a powerful salesperson, persuaded everyone else into believing it.

She also gave the illusion of her soft femininity.

This I was quicker to see through. It was the illusion my mother used to try to have me cultivate. Hairdressers were advised to fluff and curl my straight blond hair. Pastel clothes were hung like cotton candy on my back. In the end my mother would shake her head. "It's those dark eyes and eyebrows of yours," she had moaned. "They give you away." Nicole's eyes also gave her away; they were a clear, cold green.

A dowdy older woman had linked arms with her while coming through the door, chattering gaily like a mother hen. "Nicole, I know I'm just going to be thrilled with this trip."

"I'm sure you will, Mrs. Finlay," said Nicole sweetly. Was there the slightest hint of a Southern accent? "Now be sure to drop me a postcard. I want to hear what a good time you're having."

"Oh, I will, dear." Mrs. Finlay twittered her goodbye and fluttered out the door.

Nicole stared at the closed door a moment as though she contemplated kicking it, took a deep breath, and then noticed me.

"May I help you with something?" She smiled warmly.

"Thank you, I'm waiting for Mr. Garrison." She saw the application and sized me up quickly in a manner that made me uneasy. She was the kind of woman whose first impressions stuck. If she didn't like me at that moment, she never would.

The door opened again, and a leathery, country-club couple emerged followed by Scott Garrison. He was the most exciting man I'd ever seen.

There was a long, catlike grace to his movements, black hair offsetting startling blue eyes. He looked barely forty. Interesting lines had begun around his mouth and at the corners of his eyes. He might have been a typical movieland executive, but for another, more disturbing look in the depths of those eyes, something alien to that successful look. Vulnerability.

I suddenly saw him as a misplaced adventurer from another century—an Elizabethan swashbuckler who wrote love sonnets to his mistress. I pictured him in billowy white sleeves, sword in hand, against a stormy gray sky. Yet there he stood, in his Pierre Cardin suit, chatting amiably with tour customers.

While the wife hung on his every word, the leathery husband became enthralled with Nicole walking across the room. Nicole could captivate every male eye in a room, simply by walking across it. There was none of the obvious Marilyn Monroe undulation to her movements. She simply expected to captivate, and therefore did.

Mrs. Country Club was too enraptured with Scott to notice her husband's roving eye, but Scott saw everything. As Nicole passed him to return to the office, he touched her arm gently, almost imperceptibly, with an amused smile on his lips. Nicole ignored him.

I've tried to imagine how I must have looked to them all that day. Freshly scrubbed and wide-eyed, I was in a San Francisco knit dress a little too tight around the tits. I felt the white gloves would

offset the image in case my interviewer turned out
to be a woman. "Nice tits," Scott would say much
later. "You know that's why I hired you."

If he really noticed them that day, I was unaware of it. It was one of Scott's charms that he
forced you to act like a lady while every other
instinct told you to lie down and spread your legs.
And there was no difficulty conjuring up an object for a blow job. It hung slightly to the left,
bulging visibly under the well-tailored pants.

Ed Rodriguez had told me that Royal Beverly
sold the largest volume of airline tickets in California, but the room Scott led me through contained only four metal desks and a row of file
cabinets. It made the Matson Line's typing pool
look like the palace of Versailles. At the end of
this small room were two doors. One was un-
marked, and I assumed it to be a supply room.
The other read, "Scott Garrison, Vice President,
General Manager."

Scott's office was a shocking contrast to the
utilitarian atmosphere of the rest of the agency; it
contained the surroundings of a man born to
wealth, or at least expensive taste. Stark walls of
beige grasscloth set off a handsome zebra-striped
couch. There were some carved wood African
sculptures on a coffee table. On the wall behind
his desk hung an unusual painting, a cheetah on
the back of a wildebeest. It was obvious the cheetah
had attacked an animal too big to kill. The wildebeest, in a violent move, had almost thrown it
loose, though the sharp teeth were sunk deep into
that screaming animal's neck.

"Ed Rodriguez says you'd made a good travel agent," he began, pinning me with his disturbing blue eyes.

"I'd make an excellent travel agent," I said boldly, feeling my throat go dry. In my fantasy I saw him leap over the desk, shred off all his clothing except for the leopard-skin loincloth, which I'd rip off with my teeth. Then, on the zebra couch, Tarzan and I would—

"What makes you think you'd be good?"

I had no idea except that suddenly I wanted this job more than I had ever wanted anything. I thought quickly of the four metal desks that handled the largest volume of airline tickets in California, and I made my answer: "I can sell."

Without taking his eyes off me, he pressed a button on his intercom. "Ralph, I have a young lady here who wants to be a travel agent. You have a moment?"

I was ushered into the office next door I had thought was the supply room. That first guess wasn't too far wrong. Boxes of freshly printed tour brochures lined the walls and occupied the two folding chairs, which faced an old, scratched, wooden desk, also piled high with papers and files.

A small, thin man, with huge hollows for eyes, sat nearly invisible behind the large cluttered desk. This was Ralph Gordon, the owner of one of the most successful travel agencies in the United States.

He rose slightly when I entered the room, shook hands with me, then sat back down again quickly.

Scott moved one of the cardboard boxes off a folding chair for me while he remained standing.

There was an awkward silence for a moment
until Scott prompted me. "Would you like to tell
Mr. Gordon what you just told me about being a
travel agent?"

"I can sell," I said simply. My instincts told me
Ralph Gordon was a man who liked concise statements.

"Do you know ticketing?" he asked, seeming
unimpressed.

"Yes, certainly," I answered. I was surprised at
how calm and convincing my voice sounded. Ralph
was not convinced and looked to Scott for confirmation.

"I have it from Ed Rodriguez," said Scott.

Mr. Gordon's nonexistent eyebrows raised
slightly while the corners of his mouth turned
down. "You worked for Rodriguez?" he asked.

"No, but he taught me ticketing."

There was the slightest flicker of a smile behind
the corneas of those sunken eyes. "What would
you do if someone called in and wanted to know
the fare to Bangkok with stopovers in Hong Kong,
Tokyo, Manila and Vancouver?" he fired at me
like a machine gun. At the same time he moved
out from behind his desk. There was too much
energy in that small, frail body for it to stay in one
place long. He lifted a huge rate book off the floor
and handed it to me.

Did he really expect me to look up the complicated rate structure? To compute the mileage,
wade through the diagrams? I decided to answer

him honestly. "I'd call Pan Am's Rate Desk and have them figure it out."

"Rodriguez," Ralph said to Scott, and returned to his desk.

"But, Mr. Gordon," I said quickly. "You pay me to *sell* travel. Pan American can afford a whole staff of people to do nothing but figure out fares. Why waste your time with trivia that doesn't bring you in any money?"

The invisible eyebrows lifted again and there was a thin smile on Ralph Gordon's lips. He nodded to Scott, who led me out of the office.

"Starting salary is four hundred dollars a month," said Scott. "See you nine o'clock Monday morning."

6

"And I never even had time to think about giving him a blow job." I told Cindy about Mr. Gordon over dinner that night at Trader Vic's. We had gone there to celebrate my new job.

"That's a bunch of bullshit, anyway," said Cindy, already on her second Mai Tai. "Any man can get a good blow job, but he can't always find a good employee."

"Ain't it the truth," confirmed a man at the next table. We ignored him. He was one of two men, obviously conventioneers, staying at the Hilton upstairs. "Can we buy you a drink, ladies?" The other one leaned over with a large leering smile.

"Go fuck yourself," said Cindy quietly to the man, and picked up a piece of eggroll. "Men away from their wives assume every woman is a hooker," she told me. "It's best to ignore them."

"What about Bob?" I dared to ask. "Do you think he plays around when he's out of town?" He was at the moment.

She shook her head and ordered us two more Mai Tais and some Crab Rangoon. "He's not the type."

"What is the type?"

"Next table. Bob's just not a hustler, and he's

37

not that horny. I give him all the loving he needs. Why go out for hamburger when you've got steak at home?"

"Even steak every night can get dull," I suggested.

"Not if you fix it differently. Bob just isn't a player. When I was working I made it with enough married ones to pick them out."

"What's the giveaway?"

"Hungry look in their eyes. Bob doesn't have it. I've watched him at parties. He sits around, BS's with the guys, sports, Wall Street talk. He's not out to impress the ladies. Actually," she said, taking a piece of Crab Rangoon and dipping it in the sauce, "he's not very sure of himself around women. That's why he waited so long to get married."

"How'd you ever get him to propose?"

"Get *him* to propose?"

"You mean you asked him?"

"I told you he wasn't very sure of himself. I just sort of helped things along. You want to hear a good one? And I'll kill you if you ever let it out."

"Cross my heart."

"He thought I was a virgin, so we never even made it until our wedding night!"

"I think that's charming, Cindy." I tried not to laugh. "I really do. How many men in this day and age—how the hell did you pull it off?"

"Easy." She took a bite of a spare rib. "I've lost my virginity dozens of times. It really turns a guy on to think you've chosen him. You cry and whimper a lot. A tiny scream doesn't hurt, and it's best if you have your period. The blood makes it look more authentic."

"You're disgusting," I giggled. "I'm dying to try it. I've never been much good at manipulating situations with men. I should have majored in psych, like you."

"You won't find anything like that in the books," she laughed, "but you can improvise on some basic theories."

"All right, what am I going to do about this travel-agency Tarzan who's hung like a gorilla and walks like a cat?"

"Give him some pussy," offered our neighbor from the next table.

7

*When I arrived at eight-fifty-five Monday morn-*ing, Priscilla, the receptionist, motioned me grace-fully into the inner office. "She isn't paid to think," Freddy told me later. "Priscilla fills in tickets, answers phones, and acts as a buffer between us and the customers." Nonetheless, she had a lovely smile.

Nicole was going over some files at her desk. "Good," she said, looking up, "You're here on time. You're to report to me. I'm Nicole Randall. This," she said, handing me a brochure, "is our Hawaii package. Study it. When you're through, I'll give you a quiz."

It was a plain black and white brochure that had been slapped together in a moment of inspiration by Ralph Gordon. On the cover was a blurry old photo of Waikiki and the words HAWAII $235. Even the language inside failed to extol the exciting wonders of a Polynesian Paradise. It read simply.

TOUR INCLUDES:
   *Air fare, round-trip, United Airlines
   *7 days, 6 nights hotel (Waikiki)
   *Transfers
   *Flower lei greeting

The tour price of $235, in heavy black type, was the most prominent feature of the brochure.

At $235? Even at double occupancy, this was impossible. The regular air fare, economy, was two hundred dollars. Transfers from the airport were two dollars and fifty cents each way. A flower lei greeting was a couple of dollars. Where did they find a hotel for under eight dollars a night?

"The best thing is not to lie about it," advised Nicole. "The Tiki Palms is a dump, probably the biggest dump in Honolulu."

At that moment, Freddy waltzed in, sporting a tan suede jacket. In his early thirties, he retained the impish look of the little boy who just lifted a candy bar from the dimestore. The kind you couldn't resist hugging, even while he squirmed and made faces. I loved him immediately.

"You're telling her about the Tiki Tacky!" he exclaimed flinging the expensive jacket carelessly over his chair. My hopes of instant love so soon extinguished. His voice and intonations had the unmistakable bitchy whine of the gay male.

"Hi, I'm Fred." He smiled broadly at me. "Welcome aboard the good ship *Lollipop*. What sign are you?"

"Sagittarian."

"Oh! The born traveler! This business is absolutely riddled with Sagittarians. What a relief we're all going to get along so well. Nicole's an Aries. Both Scott and I are Leos. All fire signs, do you believe it? Ralph's a Taurus with Virgo rising. Yech! Helen's a—"

"Freddy," sighed Nicole, "why don't you put the coffee on?"

"That's an Aries for you." He laughed and flew off.

Freddy was in charge of the group desk. As Nicole explained, "Mr. Gordon's theory is that it takes just as much effort to book a hundred people on a single tour as it does to book one."

"That's a laugh," interjected Freddy, bringing us each a cup of coffee, "A hundred people in a group still breaks down into a hundred crotchety individuals."

Nicole told me that I would be selling the $235 package to Hawaii. Ralph Gordon ran an ad in the Sunday *Times* which, even on a slow week, would fill fifteen seats on the Saturday-morning jet to Honolulu. Nicole explained that the $235 was a giveaway. We only broke even on the land portion, but according to the rules, it made us eligible to claim ten percent commission on the air fare. Also, for each fifteen seats sold, one passenger flew free—an extra two hundred dollars in Ralph's pocket.

"Figure it out," said Nicole seriously. "Fifteen sales justify your existence. Sixteen make it worthwhile."

I had already sold two and was feeling exhilarated when Scott walked in around eleven A.M. He looked even better, if that was possible, than I had remembered him. He stopped by my desk to ask pleasantly how I was doing and if I had any questions. I proudly told him about my sales, while trying to think of something intelligent to ask him. I thought of the vouchers Nicole had shown me that morning, the official-looking slips of paper that entitled one to transfers, hotel rooms, and flower lei greetings. "If for some reason a customer doesn't use a voucher—" I asked him, "say a friend takes him to the airport—can he get a refund?"

Scott turned to Nicole, who was with a customer, then turned back to me. "Better ask Nicole when she's through." He then disappeared into his office.

At noon, Freddy popped over to my desk and invited me to lunch. "Nicole doesn't believe in taking lunch. It's against her religion."

"What religion is that?" I asked naïvely. Nicole laughed.

"Freddy refers to my religious attachment to work. You two can bring me back a tuna sandwich."

"Life's just a giggle," said Freddy as we walked out the door. "That's my philosophy of life. If you take all this too seriously, you're in big trouble," he warned me. He was also anxious to fill me in on any office gossip, beginning with Nicole.

"You'll like her," he said as we sat down at the lunch counter, "just as soon as you get to know her. Which may not be 'til next year. Smashing-looking woman, don't you think?" I nodded in agreement. "She keeps her past and present a deep dark secret, but I happen to know she's having an affair with the bank manager downstairs. You should see him. What a hump. And when I like 'em, you know they're good-looking."

I asked how he knew they were having an affair. "Well, I was on a familiarization tour one weekend given by United Airlines. Actually, I'm pretty familiar with New York. I used to live there. But it just so happened that weekend this bizarre friend of mine had a birthday—he's asexual, ever hear of such a thing? Tried women, men, everything, and I mean *every*thing. Found he just didn't like sex, so he's *a*sexual. Bizarre. Anyway, we stopped in at the St. Regis Bar to catch a glimpse of Salvador Dali, who's always there, and who should we run into? Nicole and the bank manager in the lobby. He was there on business, and she was there on a pass from the agency. She told me later, she never thought she'd run into me. After all, a city the size of New York—but that just goes to show you. Anyway, I promised I'd never tell anyone and here I've just told you. Well, it will absolutely stop there." I made a mental note never to tell Freddy anything I didn't want published in the LA *Times*.

"Ralph's an OK guy," Freddy continued with his rundown of the Royal Beverly Tour staff. "People fall into either one of two categories for him. People who make money for him, and people he can make money off of. Nobody else counts."

"What about his family?"

Freddy shrugged his shoulders. "I don't know. He's got a wife and four kids. They probably all have paper routes. Actually he's a hell of a nice

guy, if you make money for him. He's not afraid
to give a raise and drop a little extra in your paycheck when you do a particularly good job."

I was bursting to ask him. "What about Scott
Garrison?"

Freddy's dark eyes twinkled with mischief. "You
were just waiting for me to get to him!" He lowered
his voice and said ominously, "He's hung like a
donkey."

"I'm not blind, Fred. What's his situation?"

"I don't know."

"You're a veritable encyclopaedia about everyone else!"

"He's not gay, if that's what you mean, but other
than that, I don't know what he does off-hours. In
fact, I really don't know too much about what he
does on-hours. He's only been here six months.
Used to have his own agency, but I understand it
went under. Real piss-elegant-type agency. All his
clients are well-to-do. He doesn't bother with us
much. Helen thinks he lives with someone."

"Who's Helen?"

"Oh," laughed Freddy, "you haven't met Helen
yet? That's a treat. I'm not going to tell you a
thing about her. It's going to be an utter surprise."

No sooner was I settled back into my desk when
Helen Themis made her entrance. She was fond of
entrances. She flung off her large hat, did a couple
of surprisingly graceful Greek dance steps—sur-
prising for a woman of her immense size, and
made a quick lunge toward Scott, who was just
coming out of his office.

"Helen," he laughed, trying to shake her, "would you let go of my nuts?"

"Just tryin' to be friendly, you big prick!" She slapped him on the shoulder, then spied me. "You're the new girl, eh?" I nodded. "How do you do, I'm Helen Themis."

"Emily Davis."

"You speak Greek, Emily?"

"No."

"Scott, you rotten sonofabitch, I thought you was gonna get a girl in here who can speak Greek to my clients. Another beautiful girl around here is about as useful as tits on a boar hog. That pea-brained Priscilla loses more customers for me." Helen looked me over from head to toe, as a horse-buyer might do. I waited for her to open my mouth and check my teeth. "See, with the kinda business I do," she said slowly to me, in case I didn't understand, "I gotta be out of the office a lot. These Greeks, ya can't just sell 'em a ticket. They also want you to pack their luggage for them, drive 'em to the airport, and babysit their husbands 'til they get back."

"I speak Spanish," I offered, "and a little French." I remembered from somewhere that Latin languages were really based on Greek.

"Yeah?" she smiled. I noticed for the first time that she had beautiful, strong features. "Then maybe you could learn a little Greek, eh? Tell you what, honey." She took me aside. "You learn a little Greek and I'll introduce you to a shipping magnate. Like Onassis. I know lots of 'em."

I readily agreed. Besides, you don't argue with a woman that size. Freddy told me later that her husband had made a lot of money—no one quite knew how—and had provided Helen with a life of luxury until he was forced into prison on income-tax evasion. Helen had no intention of giving up her life-style, which included mink coats and a yearly trip to Greece where she collected a desk drawer full of photos of all the men she had laid. She could give you their vital statistics in inches, and how long to the minute they could keep it up. Her generosity knew no bounds. She'd give you any one of their phone numbers if you were going to be in Athens.

When her husband went to prison, Helen promptly went into the travel business. The Greek community of Los Angeles fell in love with her and gave her all their round-trip tickets to Athens. It was a large community and an enormous volume of high-commission tickets. Helen continued to live well and take her yearly pilgrimages to Greece, though now it was as the honored guest of Olympic Airways.

I was totally exhausted after my first day as a travel agent, and couldn't wait to tell Cindy all about the new job. Unfortunately, the atmosphere surrounding the Bel Air villa that night was hardly conducive to it.

8

In the month I'd lived there, Bob had managed to be home only two weeks, during which time his presence was scarcely noticed. A forceful executive at work, he molded himself into the wallpaper at home. He talked to no one but Bobby who, at that age, spoke barely intelligibly. Still, they did not seem to be an unhappy couple, and, though not demonstrative, gave each other the customary pecks on the cheek when arriving and departing.

I think Bob was relieved to have me there. It took the pressure off him to provide conversational entertainment for his wife. Each time I mentioned getting an apartment, they both became adamant that I stay, citing examples of high rents and where-else-could-you-have-a-pool-and-a-maid arguments. These were highly persuasive.

The spacious guest room on the ground floor had a charming four-poster bed, an antique rolltop desk, and a small blue velvet couch. Outside was an enclosed patio off the pool, with a chaise longue and tea table. Often, late at night, I'd sit out there and listen to the crickets with a snifter of Bob's Remy Martin cognac. Bob had exquisite taste in liquor.

That night's liquor intake was unusually high. Before-dinner cocktails preceded during-dinner

49

wine, followed by after-dinner drinks. Cindy, who almost never drank around Bob, was having doubles of everything, including the wine. She was trying to interest Bob in her latest decorating schemes, asking his opinions on fabrics, colors, and furniture design.

"How about Louis Quinze for the living room, darling?"

"Fine."

"Or maybe we should do it all Mediterranean."

"All right." Then he turned to me in desperation. "What do you think, Emily?"

"But it's *your* opinion I want, honey. I already know what Emily likes, and I'll be damned if I'm going to do the living room in Danish Modern."

It was obvious Bob was having no luck that evening fading into the woodwork. I decided to do the disappearing act instead. The crickets on my patio would be easier company.

Cindy's and Bob's room was directly above mine, but in spite of Cindy's little morning innuendoes, I never heard them. I figured if you were wealthy enough to live in Bel Air, you could afford a bed that didn't creak. This night was different.

As soon as I left their company, Cindy became loudly belligerent. I could hear her as they mounted the circular stairway to the bedroom.

"You don't give a fuck what I do to this house because you're not here enough to make a difference. You could give a shit."

"You want me to give up my job? Fine. I'll

give it up. But you'll have to give up the house. And the car. And the—"

"Oh, come off it. You're a big enough executive that you don't have to travel all the time. You could let some flunky do your work."

I listened for Bob's response, but it was either inaudible or nonexistent. Cindy continued for a while in the same vein until I heard her screaming from the bedroom. "Your bed. It's my bed, too. Who the fuck do you think you are, telling me to get out of your bed?" The door slammed. There was some muffled sobbing, then silence. I listened to the crickets and sipped my cognac slowly.

I wondered about Al—the sting, even with all my new activities, hadn't gone away. Maybe he and I would have had arguments like Cindy and Bob. Maybe worse. Cindy had told me, "Consider yourself lucky you got out when you did. What if you'd had the baby and he ran out on you?" She strongly warned me not to close myself off from love because of one bad affair. "There are a hell of a lot of good men out there, though God knows, I looked long enough to find one like Bob. I never thought I'd be so lucky, Emily. He doesn't say much, but I know he loves me. And that security is worth everything. Don't kid yourself. Love is still the most important thing in life."

I hoped I wasn't causing the dissension in Cindy's house. If she had finally been able to grab hold of some happiness, she deserved to keep it.

Freddy noticed the LA *Times* under my arm the next morning. "How can you stand to read the news, darling? It's so depressing."

"Just the classified," I apologized. "I've got to find an apartment."

He grabbed the paper from me and stuffed it in the wastebasket. "Forget this, I've got just the place for you. It's a once-in-a-lifetime steal—$120 a month, a gorgeous studio in the Hollywood Hills. A friend of mine is moving out next month. You'll love it. And it's right around the corner from me, so you can use my pool any time you want. Give me your address. I'll pick you up tonight, we'll go to dinner, then I'll show you the place."

Tension hung heavy as summer smog in the Bel Air estate that night. I was glad to have an excuse to leave. Cindy continued her harangue at Bob. "You're going to spoil that child. You never give him any discipline. He thinks I'm the ugly ogre who punishes, while you arrive home with all these presents." He had just bought Bobby an expensive swing set for the backyard. I think Cindy was just angry that, after their previous night's blow-up, she wasn't the one to get the conciliatory guilt offering.

Freddy arrived none too soon. Cindy and Bob were treating me too much like family and not enough like a guest. I was no longer being spared the family arguments. The next step, I feared, would be forcing me into the role of mediator.

Bob shook hands with Freddy, then left the room. I would have thought nothing of his departure, but Cindy whispered loudly, "Bob can't stand fags." I was afraid Freddy might have heard, and it made me angry. Bob's feelings were his own business. He at least had the good manners to keep them to himself. Social indignation nearly grabbed hold of me, but I was helpless. If Freddy hadn't heard, why bring it up? Freddy seemed agitated and anxious to leave, so we quickly departed, and I left the subject alone.

Halfway through dinner, Freddy looked up suddenly and said, "You know, I heard your cousin's remark."

"I thought you had. I'm sorry."

"You can't apologize for other people. It's not exactly the first time I've heard things like that. Most people don't bother to whisper."

"It must be difficult."

"At one time, yes," he smiled, "but not anymore. I've made my adjustments. I just didn't want you to feel badly about what your cousin said. I could see you were embarrassed."

The apartment was everything Freddy had described, but he neglected to tell me how small it was. After rattling around for a month in a Bel Air villa, could I adjust to a tiny one-room studio without a maid? Its saving grace was the large wooden sun deck, stretching the length of the apartment and providing a spectacular view of the city. I paid my deposit to the landlord and went over to Freddy's to celebrate my departure from Bel Air.

Freddy's home was one of those architectural wonders you see featured in *House and Garden*. It grew organically out of the hillside, wrapping delicately around existing trees. Skylights provided shafts of sunlight during the day, starlight at night. There were thick rust-colored carpets throughout on dark-stained hardwood floors. Ferns and spider plants hung in profusion from beamed ceilings. The furniture was soft and luxurious, ultra-modern in style. Abstract paintings, carefully chosen for complementing color and design, hung on wood-paneled walls. The swimming pool lay amidst a terraced garden, drooping with hot-colored petunias and wild rose bushes, which seemed to languish under the moonlight.

"Are you sure you wouldn't like a roommate?" I suggested. "I could learn to cook."

"Thanks, love," he said, mixing me a drink, "but I couldn't afford it."

"Afford it? I'd be happy to pay you $120 a month for the privilege of living here." I laughed.

"Sorry, darling, but with you here, I'd lose my living expenses. You don't think I bought this on the meager pittance Ralph Gordon pays us, do you?"

"You devil," I teased. "You're moonlighting on the side."

"You could call it that." He winked at me. "Actually, darling, I'm kept."

9

It was my third day at Royal Beverly and I was watching Nicole make a sale. An opera aficionado could not have been more entranced with a Beverly Sills aria.

"We want to see all the islands," the young lady announced to Nicole.

"Oh, yes," agreed her traveling companion, "a week in Waikiki, two days on Kauai, two on Maui, one in Kona, and one in Hilo."

"The outer islands are gorgeous," said Nicole enthusiastically. "It's a quiet beauty, lush greenery, long unspoiled beaches—so few tourists." She paused suddenly and looked at her clients as though for the first time. "Forget it," she said shaking her head, "I won't send you there."

The two mouths dropped open.

Nicole added in a lower voice, "Look, I adore the outer islands. They're truly lovely and my boss likes us to push them, because it's more money for the agency, but I couldn't send you there."

"Why not?" asked the two incredulous mouths in unison.

Nicole glanced around warily to see if her boss was watching. "You'd be bored stiff. Nothing's there but newlyweds and nearly-deads. The action, the young people, are all in Waikiki. The men, the night life—there isn't any night life on the outer islands. But, of course, if you really want to see the scenery, I'll be glad to book it for you." She shrugged helplessly. "Like I said, it's more money for us."

The girls looked at each other, made a quick decision, then informed Nicole they'd stay in Waikiki.

"Time," Nicole informed me after the girls left, "eats away at your profit. Booking the outer islands is a hassle, because we have no set deals with the hotels. Each one has to be reserved separately. A deposit must be sent. Flights have to be booked. Transfers are arranged with each island's tour company. In the height of the season, you can waste an hour on a single customer. It's time you could have used selling another two customers. We only make money on the outer islands when it's a large group. Then, like Ralph says, you can book twenty rooms in the time it takes to book one."

She quietly applauded me later that afternoon when I told a middle-aged couple, "I'd hate to see you go to the expense of visiting the outer islands. You can see the same scenery on a ten-dollar Circle Island Tour of Oahu. You'd be spending half your vacation packing and unpacking, checking in and out of hotels and airports. Of course my boss likes me to sell all the islands because it's more profit for us, but—"

It wasn't long before I was making over my quota of sales. Ralph was pleased and told me so by adding an extra twenty-five dollars a month to my paycheck. "Big deal," quipped Cindy. But I was learning the art of selling. I could size up a customer, persuade him to buy what *I* wanted to sell, close in at the right moment, and ask for a deposit before he could back out. I watched and learned from Nicole. It was a soft-sell technique, but highly effective.

She often told a customer, "If you haven't made up your mind, go and shop around, check out other tours. I won't guarantee that we will have space for you in a week, but I want you to be sure. You only get one vacation a year, and you deserve the best you can get for your money." That line almost always secured her a deposit. When it didn't, the customer was back a few hours later, having decided to book with Nicole because she was "honest."

To the inevitable question about the Tiki Palms, she said, "It's old and run-down. If you want a luxury hotel, I'll be happy to book it for you, but you won't get it for the price of our tour. On the other hand, we've never had a complaint about the hotel. It's smack in the center of Waikiki, only a block from the beach. It's clean and convenient, and how much time do you really spend in a hotel room?"

"I guess you could call it a negative approach," said Nicole, trying to analyze it for me. "I deliberately undersell the product. People are wary of all the commercials they see and hear every day. They think everyone's trying to take them. We come along and offer them a low-cost, no-frills product with no pretensions—we actually save them money by not booking the outer islands."

She paused for a moment, then smiled, "Scratch all that. It's worthless. When you come right down to it, it's all personal. Either they like you or they don't; either they trust you or they don't. If they don't, no package in the world is going to make your sale."

One morning I arrived an hour early to do some ticketing. Nicole, as usual, was already there, but this morning she had company. I could only see the tall man from the back, but it was Nicole's face that astounded me. I had known only the super saleswoman, efficient, friendly. This morning she was all coquette, flirting and feminine, a veritable Scarlett O'Hara, captivating and younger than I'd ever seen her.

"Seven o'clock tonight, Mrs. Randall," said the man, "and you'd better not stand me up again."

"There's no telling what I'll do," she laughed, delighted to provoke him. She saw me come in and quickly changed her expression. "Oh, Mr. MacCallister, I'd like you to meet our new employee, Miss Emily Davis."

Mr. MacCallister turned and I saw an attractive, confident, and powerfully built man in his late forties. He was the type who had played football in college, and jogged every morning to keep in shape. As Nicole told me later, "He'll give you two ups for one down."

"Mr. MacCallister is the manager of the bank downstairs," continued Nicole, "He handles our business. You might want to open your own account there. It's very convenient and the service is excellent." Her eyes twinkled while he threw her a smile. The crossfire was becoming uncomfortable. I tried to think of a graceful exit when Scott Garrison walked in and provided it for me. He issued a curt, "Morning, Jack, Nicole." Then: "Emily, may I see you a moment in my office?"

His voice had the tone of a boss who was about to tell you you're canned. I was petrified, trying to remember what I'd done wrong. I walked into his office slowly. "Close the door, will you, please?" he said and leaned up against his desk. He lit a cigarette silently, blew the smoke out, and looked at me steadily out of his deep blue cat eyes. My arms were two feet too long and my legs couldn't decide how to place themselves. I knew he was aware of my discomfort, even enjoying it. A cat would rather play with its prey than kill it right off. I attempted a smile and to my surprise, he returned it.

"Am I that funny?" I asked.

"Yes," he grinned. His eyes were alive, but he remained still, watching me.

"I'm taking you to lunch today," he announced finally, as though it had taken a long time to reach that conclusion.

"Now don't just stand there with that simple expression on your face," he laughed. "Go out there and sell something."

It took centuries to reach noon, and then another half-hour of eternity before Scott left his office. Nicole looked up briefly as we left and Freddy gave me a mischievous—or was it lewd?—wink.

For a girl who usually radiates self-confidence, I was, for the first time in my life, feeling like a

teenager on her first date. I wanted badly to impress Scott with some glib conversation, but words
only stuck in the back of my throat, emerging
intermittently as strange, inaudible sounds that I
hardly recognized as my own voice. So acutely
aware was I of my own discomfort, I hardly
noticed Scott was also ill at ease. It was obvious,
though unsaid, that this was the first step toward a
flirtation or an affair. Even animals have their
primitive courting rites; people use small talk.

"What made you decide to go into the travel
business?" he asked me.

"It seemed like a good idea for a career," I
answered. "Why did you get into it?"

"What are you escaping?" he asked, quickly
avoiding my question.

The liquor was beginning to loosen my throat.
"An unfortunate love affair." I thought that would
sound intriguing, but he laughed. I must not have
pulled it off convincingly. Actually, the more time
I spent with Scott, the less unfortunate my affair
with Al seemed.

"So you came to LA to find yourself another
unfortunate love affair?" he flirted.

"No. I came here to seek my fortune."

"They only do that in fairy tales. In real life,
most people spend their time like you do, trying to
escape the sordid details of their pasts. Travel
agents are the worst—or the best—at it."

"Why's that?"

"We have so many practical options open to us."

The waiter picked up my plate, and I gazed
with horror at the glaring, pink, Thousand Island—

dressing blotches my sloppy eating habits had left on the white tablecloth. The French bread I had buttered had shed a circle of crumbs marking the exact spot my plate had been. I was raised with ladylike table manners; they just never took. Scott's place was clean.

"How do you like your job?" he asked.

"There's so much to learn. I never thought the business world would be so complex. College was a snap in comparison."

"You'll end up back in college," he said knowingly.

I thought back on the cold gray buildings of the Cal campus, the uncomfortable desks, dry, meaningless lectures on useless subjects, card catalogues, term papers, final-exam blue books. The Royal Beverly office flashed through my mind, with its frantic ticket deadlines, anxious tour customers, sales pressures. I thought of the trips I would take to the colorful places I was selling. "No, I don't think I'll ever go back to school."

"You'll change your mind," he said definitively. "I did."

This was the closest I got that afternoon to any reference to his personal life. He skillfully detoured around my questions. At the end of two hours and several drinks, I knew no more about Scott Garrison than Freddy had told me.

Nicole greeted me coldly back at the office. "Mr. Gordon doesn't like us to take more than an hour for lunch," she said. "Scott Garrison works here on commission, so what he does is on his own time. You're on Mr. Gordon's payroll." I apologized,

went to my desk, then turned livid with rage. Had
she already forgotten the extra hour I'd put in that
morning on my own time? No, Nicole wasn't one
to overlook a detail. A few moments later she
stopped by my desk. Her tone of voice had softened. "I don't mean to be hard on you, Emily.
You've been doing an excellent job and I appreciate the extra time you're putting in. It's just that
the noon hours are often the busiest in a travel
agency. It's the only time some of our clients have
to talk about their trips and pick up tickets."

"I'll watch it from now on. I just didn't realize—"

"I know you didn't." She smiled. "But now you
do."

10

"*Would you water my plants over the weekend,* darling?" asked Freddy the next morning, dropping his house key on my desk. "I'm going up to Frisco."

"*San* Francisco." I corrected him out of a sense of duty to my home town.

"If you ask me, that's what's wrong with the city," commented Nicole. "People there are trying to protect a phony dignity, a way of life that's obsolete, while the rest of the world is forging ahead. Anyone with imagination moved down here, where they wouldn't have to waste time protecting precious traditions."

"I don't care what you say," defended Freddy, "It's still the only city in the world you can get laid four times in one night."

"Even if you could attract it," said Helen skeptically, "you couldn't get it up that much. Though God knows, there ain't much to get up."

"Everything being relative, Helen," countered Freddy, "you need a manhole cover for a diaphragm."

"Hard hat, hard cock," shrugged Helen. "Hey, you ever laid a hard-hat, Nicole?"

"It's nice to have all those muscles," sighed

Nicole, "but it takes more than that to be a good lover."

"Like what?" asked, Scott who had just entered the room.

"Like a good strong back," laughed Nicole.

"Why's that?" he smiled.

"I don't like to always be on top."

The smile left his face and he turned to me. "And what do you prefer, Emily? Top or bottom?"

There were sparks of electricity flashing between us. I flushed crimson. Top or bottom? I'd never even considered the problem. With Al, it had been a victory to catch him off enough pills to perform. Scott was staring at me, waiting for an answer. I shrugged and threw the question back to him. "What do *you* prefer?"

"I prefer to be in love," he answered slowly, caressing each word for me with only a hint of sarcasm. Our eyes clung together boldly for a long moment.

So this was big-game hunting. I wasn't clear which was the hunter—or the huntee.

"The fucker or the fuckee," Cindy corrected me later.

"He scares the pants off me," I said.

"That's an apt expression," she noted. "Obviously you're going to have an affair with the man."

"I'm not sure I want to."

"After everything you've told me, you don't *want* to? Or you're just afraid you're going to get hurt again. Look, when you start to walk as a child, you fall down a lot at first, but that doesn't mean you decide, on that basis, to spend the rest of your life crawling on all fours."

Having the key to Freddy's house while he was gone finally gave me the opportunity to show it to Cindy. After her comment about "fags" that night, I couldn't very well ask Freddy to give her a house tour. Still, I was dying to hear her reaction to the extraordinary home.

"I don't like it," she announced adamantly one step inside Freddy's front door. "Outside, with all that wood and landscaping, it's quite nice, but inside, he's ruined it. Colors are too hot—all these rusts and oranges. It's dark and decadent. These hanging plants make it look like a teeming swamp. Definitely a fag pad, overdone, excessive, perverted, demented."

"Oh, come off it, Cindy. It's like preferring ice cream to cake."

"It's a sickness, Emily." She gestured around the house. "This is neurotic. You can feel it permeating, dripping off the walls."

"You're out of your mind. It's a lovely house, just a little unusual."

"Stay away from him," warned Cindy ominously, "or you'll get labeled a fag hag. You should hear my husband on the subject. Says fags are men who just don't have the guts to take on a real woman."

"Maybe it takes more guts to approach a man," I suggested. "After all, you could get hurt. A lot of them swing both ways, you know. I wouldn't be surprised to learn Freddy did. In fact," I added just to shock her, "maybe I'll have an affair with him."

"I wouldn't hold my breath waiting for him to stick it in you, and if he does, I hope you know they're quite fond of fanny fucking. Just don't ever bring him around my place again. Bob would as soon as kill any of those perverts who ever laid a hand on his son."

"Bobby's only two."

"Children are very impressionable. They're better off not exposed to that sort of thing at all."

I thought about Cindy's comments when I saw Freddy Monday morning. I had certainly been attracted to him at first, but the thought of an affair hadn't consciously occurred to me before I said so to Cindy. I hadn't known many homosexuals, and wondered how purist they were. Could a man really turn off all desire for a woman? I tried to imagine myself with a woman. No, the soft, smooth curves of a woman's body held no appeal for me. How did one get attracted to a person of the same sex?

It had been months since my abortion, and though I was faithfully taking The Pill, I chose to remain celibate. There had been some casual dates, and I once even considered giving Ed Rodriguez a sort of "thank you" fuck for recommending the job at Royal Beverly. There was no danger of falling in love with him, but since I was only marginally attracted to him, I concluded it wasn't worth the effort. But Scott Garrison—he was making tidal waves in my bloodstream.

Nicole interrupted my thoughts. "How about

lunch today?" I was shocked. Nicole taking lunch? And with me?

We went to a crowded little Swedish sandwich shop around the corner on Rodeo. "I've seen a lot of girls come through this place in ten years," she told me halfway through the open-faced sandwich, "but you're the only one who's really been able to cut the mustard. You have business ability. That's unusual, even with intelligent girls."

I returned the compliment and told her how much I admired her work. "Have you ever thought of owning your own agency?" I asked her.

"Of course. It's a big responsibility. You've got to really know what you're doing or you can lose your shirt. Like what happened to Scott Garrison." Before I could ask her the details, she kept on going. "There's not much money in a travel agency, unless you run it right and know how to invest the money you make. What about you, Emily? You want to own your own agency or just find a nice guy, settle down and have babies?"

"Thanks, I just had a baby, so to speak. I think I'd rather run a business at the moment than run a family." I sighed. "I seem to have more luck at work than I have at love."

There was a smile of recognition. "I know the feeling," she said. "Where'd you have the abortion, Mexico?" I nodded, and she shook her head. "At least now you're in the travel business you can go to Japan or Sweden. In fact, if you're ever in need again, I know a good gynecologist in the Valley."

It suddenly occurred to me that this was the first

personal exchange Nicole and I had ever had. She was no longer the boss lady addressing an employee. I told her about Al, and she winced sympathetically. "I don't think you can ever love again with the painful intensity you feel at that age," she said, and began telling me about her life.

Nicole had been raised in a Catholic orphanage in New Orleans. Her father, whom she no longer remembered, had dropped her off there when she was three. She had spoken only French. "Since I couldn't understand what they were saying, the kids loved to torment me. They were very cruel, and I spent a good part of my childhood beating them up to win their respect. I was a mean, angry brat, and I guess that's why nobody adopted me for a long time. Finally, an ex-chorus girl who had made a respectable fortune in the restaurant business, and a sizable contribution to the orphanage, took me home. She liked the feistiness in me. I disliked her at first as much as anyone, but it was a way out of the orphanage and the strict nuns.

"At eighteen she caught me in bed with the restaurant dishwasher. She wasn't angry or even surprised. He was young and good-looking, but she thought he was a waste of my time. I was really quite a beauty, especially when I was dressed up. She put me to work as a hostess, where I'd attract some of her higher-class clientele.

"One night the man of my dreams walked in—a young doctor. Oh, was he handsome. Took your breath away. He fell head over heels in love, married me within a month. I learned to cook like a French chef, entertained his friends elegantly. We had a large house with a pool. It was like living in a fairy tale." Nicole's voice trailed off into the mist, then her eyes narrowed.

"The day I came home from the hospital with our baby girl, he sat on the edge of my bed and told me he wanted a divorce. He was head over heels in love with another woman, a pediatrician. I got into the car with my baby, dropped her off at the orphanage where I was raised, checked into a motel, and slit my wrists.

"When I came around several months later, I was in a mental hospital. It was the old lady, my adopted mother, who had gotten through to me. I remember her saying, 'Honey, there's only two kinds of men in this world: those that are good for shit, and those that aren't good enough for shit. You gotta learn to take care of yourself.' "

"What happened to your baby?"

"She's fine," said Nicole calmly, though I could see the pain deep inside her eyes. "She lives with her father and his wife—the pediatrician."

"Have you seen her?"

"No. They told her I was dead."

"And you never contacted her to—"

"What good would it do?" said Nicole bitterly. "She's better off with them. I was pretty unstable in those days. I'd have been an awful mother. They love her. It's their only child. They never could have one of their own. The pediatrician always felt guilty about the whole affair. She's kept contact with me secretly, sends me photos. Jeanne's sixteen now, going to graduate from high school soon. That's the only thing I wish—perhaps—

somehow to attend her graduation. I missed all the birthdays and things."

Nicole picked up the tab for lunch over my protests. "Save your money," she joked. "You don't make enough yet to be blowing it. I'll give you another couple of months and you can treat me to lunch at the Polo Lounge."

11

To some out-of-towners, all they know of Los Angeles, and perhaps all they care to know, is the Beverly Hills Hotel and its famous Polo Lounge. Of course, it's not the same now that Tony's gone. He had the flourish to pull it off, the familiarity combined with a respectful distance, an appealing charm tempered with authority. You always knew he was in charge and it made you feel secure. Best of all, Tony knew exactly who was screwing whom in any sense of the word, and kept his mouth shut about it. I learned all this the night Scott took me there.

Nicole, Freddy, and I had been working late, finishing the mound of tickets Priscilla had left on her desk. One hundred fourteen passengers would be waiting at the LA Airport at nine the next morning for these tickets, but that never bothered Priscilla, who left promptly every evening at five PM.

Scott was also working late with a client. Freddy recognized her as a famous Forties musical star. Her face had been pulled back several times into a tight lift under a platinum wig, and she was resplendent with jewels and lavender eye shadow.

"What do you say to these old broads?" moaned Scott after she left. "She doesn't have any cash and

71

insists upon a luxury cruise. She's living in a tinsel-town fantasy world and can't figure out why I won't extend her personal credit."

"She was one hell of a tap-dancer in her day," noted Freddy sadly.

"Maybe she'll tap-dance naked on your chest in return for the tickets," sniped Nicole.

"Smartass," said Scott, smiling at her. She looked up and smiled back. There was a pleasant warmth between them I'd never seen before.

"Hey, you old broads," he said brightly, "why don't we all go up to the Polo Lounge for a drink?"

"Sorry, darling," said Freddy, filling in the last ticket, "but I've got a tuxedo to rent and a prom to go to."

"Make sure she gives you a wrist corsage," advised Scott. "They don't get in the way if you want to dance close. What about the rest of you?"

"I've got a date," said Nicole, "but thanks anyway." He looked at her strangely for a moment, a fierce glitter in his blue eyes. When he turned to me it was gone.

"How about you, Emily?"

I didn't want to be the consolation prize, but I've never had any principles when it came to these matters. I always accepted the last-minute date to a dance, even though I may have been second choice. It was better than sitting home, and besides, I'd never been to the Polo Lounge.

Hell will freeze over before San Francisco allows one of its major hotels to be painted pink. This, however, was Beverly Hills. Tucked comfortably amidst lush greenery, the Beverly Hills Hotel re-

laxes in a perpetual sunbath at the foot of Cold-
water Canyon. Movie stars and their agents, di-
rectors, politicians, athletes, glide through the
gracious lobby on a billowy pink cloud of easy
laughter and kisses on the cheek.

Tony hugged Scott, as do Italians who haven't
seen someone since yesterday, and repeated my
name as if it belonged to a celebrity. No wonder
people loved him, loved his Polo Lounge.

We were seated at a back booth with a view of
the bar and the front door. I learned later that
these were the choice tables, where you could see,
but not be seen unless you wanted. In the next
booth a man ordered a telephone plugged in, and
loudly placed a call to London.

Our drinks were brought to the table along with
a platter of the house hors d'oeuvres.

"How do you like the place?" asked Scott, making a slight effort at conversation.

"I think I could live here quite comfortably the
rest of my life," I answered.

"Good. I'll see if I can't get you a bungalow by
the pool."

In spite of his good humor, I detected a sadness
about Scott. A well-bred politeness dictated that
he not be inattentive, but his mind was somewhere
else. Perhaps it was in this room, but with someone
else. My ego wouldn't stand for it. I looked at him
intently, forcing his eyes into mine. "My God,
you're good-looking," I said softly. "They must
think you're a movie star here."

It threw him off-guard, but lightened his spirits.
He looked at me carefully and took a sip of his

drink. "You're full of shit." He smiled. "That's why you're so good at selling."

"I'm not full of shit. You have an incredibly handsome face, a beautiful body. I bet you were the star jock of your high school."

"I never went to high school." He ran a finger across my lips. I bit it lightly and he laughed.

"You said you went to college."

"I did. Northwestern. Emily Davis, you have the most wanton eyes of any woman I've ever known."

"But Scott, how did you get to college without a high-school diploma?"

"I cheated," he smiled. I explored the contours of his long fingers with my lips. "I was stuck in boarding school at ten. Hated it. By thirteen I made my escape, if you will." Our eyes flashed at what was now our private joke. "Lied about my age to join the Merchant Marines. A few years later I decided to reconcile with my father and went home. He shoved me back into a boarding school, so I split again, came out here to California, bummed around doing odd jobs at the Marina until I was of age, then joined the Air Force. Stayed there long enough to learn to fly, then made up my mind to get a college education.

"Since I had no credentials, I started making it with the girl who gave the achievement tests. I was banging her in one room while my buddy, a pilot who held a degree from NYU, took my exam in the next room."

"You didn't have any trouble keeping up with the other kids?"

"I've always read a lot. I think I was actually

ahead of most of my freshman class. Probably could have passed the achievement test if I'd taken it. Your eyes are amazing, Emily. I'd like to fuck your eyes."

"I'd like—" How I wanted to tell him, but a stronger urge overtook me. "To find a bathroom," I blurted out. I had consumed four drinks. My angry bladder was screaming at me.

The cruel, demented chauvinist fiend who designed the Beverly Hills Hotel placed the ladies' room clear across the lobby and up a flight of stairs. It's no small feat of endurance to dash madly across an elegant lobby and maneuver a flight of stairs when you're just this side of smashed and fighting to rein in a flash flood.

To further complicate my life, I made a wrong turn on leaving the ladies' room which led me down a jungle highway hideously wallpapered with giant man-eating plants. A housekeeper recognized the symptoms of my dilemma and steered me back to the Polo Lounge.

Scott was paying the check. "I figured you were lost."

"Didn't you for even a tiny second think I might have ditched you for some super-star I'd taken up with between here and the bathroom?"

"No." He smiled, and I could see that in the time I'd left him, the sadness had returned. He was quiet when we got back into his car. After we'd driven to the office, he pulled up next to my VW in the parking lot and let me out. "See you Monday morning," he said in a businesslike manner. My insides were caving in, and it must have shown on my face, because he softened and kissed me lightly on the cheek. "Good night, Emily."

"Good night, Scott. Thank you." *Thanks for nothing, you asshole*, I thought, as I gunned my VW out of the parking lot.

12

I was still feeling angry and horny when I awoke the next morning to the telephone ringing. It was Freddy.

"What are you doing?"

"Masturbating," I yawned.

"Darling, I'd love to come over there and help you, but I'm all fucked out. Met the cutest little hump of a Mexican last night at the Baths."

"What's the Baths?"

"Oh, it's this terrific place. You go in, they give you a towel, and they have an orgy room, and a lot of little private rooms to play in."

"How exciting." I yawned again.

"Well it was obviously more thrilling than your evening with Mr. Garrison, or you wouldn't be up at this hour on a Saturday morning playing with yourself."

"Oh, Freddy," I sighed, "I think I'm going to cry. You ever see his hands? He's got the most sensuous long fingers I've ever seen."

"You can tell more about a man by looking at his forearm. Now put your bikini on and get your ass over here. You'll feel much better after a Bloody Mary or two."

"Freddy, tell me honestly. Do I have bad breath? Do I need a mouthwash?"

"You really want an honest opinion?"

"Yes."

"You're using the wrong douche."

I watched Freddy across the patio with a pitcher of Bloody Marys. There were no feminine mannerisms in his movements, only his voice. It was the thin, taut body of a swimmer with broad shoulders and muscled thighs, a tan body whose owner cared for it. Freddy once described to me the type of man's physique that turned him on. He was unaware that he described his own. When I pointed that out to him, he replied, "Don't think I've never considered fucking myself."

"You ever had a woman?" I asked him as he handed me a glass.

"Hasn't everyone?"

"I haven't."

"Nobody's perfect, darling. Work on that douche. Strawberry flavor's very big now." He took my drink, set it carefully on a table, then threw me into the pool. "There, you need cooling off," he laughed. "I had more faith in you, Emily." He dove in after me. "If I had a pussy there'd be no stopping me." He emerged from the water and swam with strong even strokes, barely disturbing the water around him. There was sensuality in the cool sleek body gliding by me.

"You don't look hampered to me," I argued, making reference to his house.

He pulled himself out of the pool. The morning sunlight reflected golden off his tanned body. "With a pussy, you can get it tied up legally, cemented with a couple of kids. A womb is a definite advantage in this racket." He moved the chaise longue out to face the sun, then dropped lazily into it. "I don't have it too bad. The house is in my name, the car—but I have no insurance against old age. Someday I'll lose my girlish figure and boom! I'm out of the running."

"I want to hear about the women you've laid," I said, climbing out of the pool.

He laughed and squinted up at me. My breasts, blossomed out from The Pill, were poking voluptuously over the top of my bikini. Even with lesser tits to my credit, my bikinied body had never failed to elicit the rapt attention of any post-adolescent male within a half-mile radius. Could Freddy, avowed as he was, remain unaffected, unmoved?

"Would it surprise you to know I have two children?"

"How virile of you. Where are they?"

"Vermont. One's legal, the other—his mother got married before he was born. I saw him a couple of years ago. A little mirror of me. Wow, what an ego trip."

"So you were married, too?"

"Shotgun. I was only seventeen. It got so out of hand that I ran off to New York and joined the Navy."

"And that's where you decided you preferred men?"

"No, I was too busy being a frogman in Korea. It wasn't until later when I came out here to LA.

"Don't get me wrong, I have nothing against women," he sat up and rubbed some suntan lotion on his chest, "it's just that I find a man's body more exciting. I like hard muscles and hairy chests—and I love to suck cock. There are few pleasures in the world that come close to a good stiff cock."

"Now tell me honestly, Freddy, are men really better at it than women?"

"On the whole, yes," he said after some consideration, "though I had this one Korean girl who specialized in blowjobs. Even had her front teeth removed for it. But men naturally know what feels good."

Here's my chance, I thought. (At this point in history, if you recall, a girl like me couldn't get hold of many books on the subject.) "What feels good?" I asked him.

"If you had a cock I'd show you," he laughed.

"Just *tell* me, before I'm overcome with an attack of penis envy."

"Well, first," he held an imaginary penis in front of him, trying to conjure up the object of his delight, "you've got to keep it really wet, and keep running your hand up and down." I was watching studiously when he looked up at me. "Haven't you ever gone down on a guy before?"

I decide to be honest. "This guy I used to go with, Al—he's actually the only lover I've ever had—I asked him once while we were making love if he liked oral sex."

"And?"

"Well, he said 'yes' and kissed me."

Freddy laughed so hard he fell into the pool. When he came out, he mixed up another pitcher of

Bloody Marys and gave me a half-hour lecture full of vivid, colorful details on the subject of fellatio. At last I was confident that if the situation ever arose, so to speak, I could carry it off like a pro. Or at least as well as any toothless Korean girl.

That afternoon spun softly into evening. Freddy and I barbecued steaks and watched winter sunset turn the gray-green Hollywood Hills golden. Not even the ocean's violent crash of waves sounds as primitive as these hills at night. Wooden homes cling tentatively onto the cliffs and dark canyons. Packs of wild coyotes live well here off rabbits and occasionally someone's plump housecat. At night howling coyote symphonies echo through the canyons. In the dry desert heat of summer, Santa Ana winds from the south rip through dense, overgrown chaparral, spreading fierce brush fires across the hills. People often wake to see deer grazing on the front lawn, nibbling rose bushes.

Freddy and I went skinny-dipping in his pool by moonlight and dried off by the fireplace. Numb with drink and sunburn, we slipped into his huge bed and fell asleep naked in each other's arms.

In the lavender-blue light of early dawn I awoke, my body pressed warmly against his, a sober rush of desire darting through me. I had never slept naked with a man before, without even the attempt of sex.

At that moment he twisted onto his back. I rested a hand on his chest, then slid it down lightly until I felt the soft hair of his groin, and finally the cock lying relaxed on his leg. He opened his eyes lazily and smiled. I began to stroke.

Without a word, he removed my hand, turned me around, wrapped his arms firmly around my chest. He dropped a heavy leg between mine and whispered in my ear, "Go back to sleep, Emily."

It occurred to me the next morning, over blueberry pancakes, that Freddy had never once expressed any panic that his jealous lover might have caught us in bed together.

"No chance of that," said Freddy, flipping the pancakes. "He's a man of regular habits. Tuesdays, Wednesdays, and Thursdays. That's all."

"How can you be sure?" I was skeptical. After all, my life might have been at stake. What a sordid death. I imagined my poor father reading about it in his beloved evening paper.

"I'm sure," he laughed. "You want maple syrup or blueberry?"

"Blueberry. But I still don't see how you can be so confident about a guy who's keeping you. Isn't that almost like a marriage?"

"Not quite, darling," laughed Freddy. "He's already married."

13

I was beginning to suspect a sadistic god named Irony was running my life. For months I had studiously avoided sex, and in one weekend I had found two men I desired. Neither one wanted me and both I would have to face at the office Monday morning.

"Hey, honey." Helen winked at me. "Hear you went out with the Big Prick Friday night. How was he, eh?"

"Not bad," I said blandly. "I've had better."

"Nothing like a big prick, I always say," added Freddy, glancing over at me.

"How would you know?" laughed Helen. "You're hung like a stud bee."

"No, he isn't," I heard myself say, "he's hung beautifully." As I said this, Scott walked in the door.

"Who's hung beautifully?" he asked.

"Freddy," said Helen. "Looks like your big prick got competition."

He looked from me to Freddy, who was smiling mischievously, then walked into his office.

"Ya hear that, Nicole?" said Helen with admiration. "This girl had both of them over the weekend. Some action." Nicole was at the adding machine and evidently didn't hear.

"I was lying," I told Helen.

"About which one?" she asked.

The buzzer on my desk rang before I could answer her. It was Scott. He wanted to see me in his office.

"Now, tell me the truth," he said, grinning. "Did you really go to bed with Freddy?"

I seated myself on his zebra couch and smiled up at him. "Yes."

"You're blushing."

"No, I'm not."

"You're lying."

"What business is it of yours?"

"You going to dinner with me tonight?"

"No."

"Did you really sleep with Freddy?"

"Yes. Why don't you believe me?"

"Come here."

I walked over to him, unshakable in my truth. After all, I did go to bed and sleep with Freddy. Scott leaned down and kissed me. It wasn't a long kiss, but it was full of promise. "Did you really fuck Freddy?"

"No."

"I didn't think so." He laughed. "Pick you up about seven. Dress for San Francisco."

I felt everyone's eyes on me when I walked out of Scott's office. Maybe my slip was hanging. Maybe my underpants. I was undone, flustered, in love. And it had only been one kiss.

I barely had time to get home, bathed and changed for my date. I thought about what Scott said, dressing for San Francisco. I slipped into a low-cut black knit dress and threw on a string of pearls.

Within twenty minutes Scott and I were at the Hollywood-Burbank airport boarding a flight to San Francisco. At the time, I figured he must have gotten some PSA passes, but I was wrong. He had paid full price for reserved tickets.

As we approached the City, I had a faint pit-of-the-throat apprehension. What if I should run into my parents? But what would they be doing out on the town on a Monday night?

We had dinner at the lovely Mandarin Restaurant in Ghirardelli Square. The owner, a Chinese woman, greeted Scott with the same pleasure and familiarity Tony had shown us at the Polo Lounge. Our table overlooked the bay, which sparkled with lights from Sausalito. We laughed and flirted through dinner, and when no one was looking, he slid his hand up my dress. I might have risked my reputation if he'd really wanted me there. Fortunately for my good San Francisco name, he had other, more intriguing plans.

"I want to show you my favorite place in San Francisco," he said as we left the restaurant. I envisioned a bridal suite at the Fairmont, but he was leading me through Aquatic Park and onto the "Historic Ships" pier.

I had been on these ships once before in my life. My father had taken me here when I was little and told me stories about how he had worked his way around the Pacific on a cargo ship when he was young. The lure of the sea and its romantic adventures thereafter figured greatly in my imagination. From our home, I used to watch the ships sail in and out of the Golden Gate, dreaming about the day they would take me to the far corners of the world.

All romantic seagoing notions, however, were quickly dashed when I took a student ship, actually an old World War II naval transport, home from Europe. We were nine days across the turbulent Atlantic Ocean with no stabilizers. I was seasick the entire trip.

The wind ripped through our hair as we walked down the pier. Foghorns sounded across the bay. "Sorry, the ships are closed for the night," said the guard coming toward us. "Oh, Scott Garrison!" He extended a friendly hand. "Didn't recognize you— go on in." He opened the gate for us.

"Thanks, Joe." Scott was the type of man who maintained a special rapport with maitre d's and armed guards. And it wasn't simply the money he slipped them for their favors. I think they truly liked him and would have helped him out for nothing.

"All the life and spirit of San Francisco is right here," he said on board the schooner. He sniffed the air like a thoroughbred and walked to the edge of the deck. The fog was creeping in under the Golden Gate Bridge. Wooden masts creaked above, pointing to the stars. Scott's black hair was blowing about his face; his blue eyes reflected the lights from Russian Hill. "Imagine they're really campfires of the miners," he whispered.

"Or the Spaniards," I suggested.

He looked very much the Spanish Conquistador.

"You've caught the spirit." He pulled me close. "History is everything—a sense of the past." His eyes glowed enthusiastically.

I desperately tried to work up his enthusiasm for history, but it reminded me of Al. This moment in time was infinitely more exciting than what happened here one hundred years ago.

"You know I was a history major in college," he said. My heart dropped like an anchor to the bottom of the bay. Not another one. "I guess it's why I went into the travel business," he continued. "History is so much a part of sightseeing, why people travel thousands of miles. The first historian, in fact, was really just writing a travelogue."

"Herodotus," I said bleakly. Al's hero. I had said the magic word for Scott. He suddenly kissed me.

"You're the first girl I ever met who knew about Herodotus!"

We walked through the ship while Scott pointed out things of interest. The captain's cabin was roped off, but we stepped over it. The carved wood paneling was freshly polished. "Beautiful, isn't it?" He turned to me. "They keep it up, just like it was still in use."

"Probably better than the captain kept it," I remarked. We sat down on the bed and looked around. The ship rocked gently; there were foghorns in the distance. Scott looked very like a sea captain in the semidarkness. "Do you think he ever had women in here?" I giggled.

"I imagine so." He reached behind me and unzipped my San Francisco black knit dress.

"It's such a small bed," I mumbled through his kisses.

Salt cold air filled the cabin; masts creaked above in rhythm with the waves lapping against the side of the schooner. Scott's long fingers turned into sensuous claws, scratching smooth patterns down my skin.

"You a good fuck?" he pulled me on top of him.

"Oh yes," I was out of breath.

"Then good-fuck me."

I gave him all the pent-up fury I'd been saving for months, until my knees were raw. Scott was orchestrating me into a frenzy. I was a beautiful animal, wild and primitive. He turned me around and sank his teeth into the skin below my neck. His powerful arms were tight about my chest. The cheetah's fangs buried in the neck of the wildebeest. We plunged deeper into our mysterious transformation. Spinning, whirling forces of energy, bursting, screaming, into the night.

"The human body is a wondrous thing," he whispered as we lay quiet. Warm caresses kept off the icy cold that threatened our wet skin.

"But you have the body of a cat." I stroked the long graceful muscles of his back. "My God, what an extraordinary fuck!"

He raised my face so I could see his eyes. "It was more than a fuck," he said. For a brief second it was there again, the vulnerability. I ran my fingers through his thick dark hair. He jerked away. "Cut with this extraneous bullshit."

I held my hand still as though he'd rammed a knife through it. He saw my hurt and kissed me lightly. "I didn't mean that," he lied. "Go ahead. It's all right." I finished the motion through his hair, then held my hands still.

"You realize this is my first shipboard romance?"

"That's what the travel business is all about," he answered.

"But I have a confession to make to you, Scott."

"Don't tell me," he teased. "You're not a virgin."

"No, Scott, this is more serious."

"I can take it."

"I prefer traveling by air."

"That could be arranged. We are travel agents, you know."

"Then you're not angry?"

"Perhaps it's one of those little things we'll never resolve. Tell me what you don't like about an ocean voyage."

"Horny ship captains, for one. They're quite a nuisance. And it takes too long to get anywhere. If we'd taken a plane we'd have been there by now. I bet we haven't even gotten out of the bay yet."

"Where're we going?"

I shrugged my shoulders.

"But you're in a hurry to get there." He glanced at his watch and began putting on his clothes. "That's the trouble with the whole world. It's in too big a hurry to get somewhere. In fact, that's the trouble with Ralph Gordon's fucking travel agency. No time to spend with a customer. Sell quick and sell a lot."

"But how can you make any money spending time with a customer?" I asked him, fumbling around the dark cabin for my shoes. It suddenly occurred to me that there might be rats scurrying around on this ship, and I wondered where rats went when they deserted a sinking ship.

"You've been indoctrinated by Nicole Randall," he said almost angrily. "Neither Nicole Randall nor Ralph Gordon has any sense of history." I watched the careful way he tucked in his shirt, folding it on each side. He then pulled his cock straight up and zipped his pants. "No sense of tradition. The romance and adventure of a vacation—the historic significance of the place they sell has no meaning in their limited definition of the travel industry."

"But they are successful," I argued.

"If making money is success to you."

We were walking past the cable car turnstile at the edge of the park near the Buena Vista Café— all turn-of-the-century landmarks. "San Francisco is at least in touch with her own past. It's not all making money."

"Though she does make a fair amount off her preoccupation with history." I pointed to the crowd of tourists bulging from the cable car.

"Granted. But there is some value system here other than profit. Los Angeles is a lady without a past or a future. Just an interminable present."

"In which to have a good time."

"A rollicking good time," he agreed sourly.

By the time we boarded our bright pink and orange jet back to Burbank, a frost had descended upon us. I hadn't meant to make a serious argument of our verbal sparring. Somehow, it had touched him. We sat in silence on what PSA calls their "Grinning Bird."

"Emily, forget this all happened," he said to me at my apartment door. I touched his hand, and he pulled it away as though I'd stuck him with a hatpin.

"You run hot and cold like a goddamn shower," I shouted and slammed the door.

14

The next day at work I decided to approach him as a friend. He might have a logical explanation for his erratic behavior. I would be mature and give him the opportunity to explain himself.

The door to his office was ajar. I took a deep breath, lifted my chin half an inch, and entered. Suddenly the entire night flashed before me as though it were my entire life and I was about to drown. The bruise on my back, where his teeth had been, gave me a sharp pain.

I stood in the doorway waiting for him to ask me in. But he appeared to be absorbed in some work. Cats often ignore you when you try to attract their attention.

I walked briskly to his desk. He looked up. I had seen Scott Garrison confident. I had seen him loving, tender, passionate, violent, angry, sarcastic, and playful. This was the first time I saw him embarrassed.

I dropped my maturity and my chin to the floor, muttered a flustered "Hi. Just thought I'd say hi," and left.

For the next several weeks, pleasant cordialities were exchanged when we were unavoidably face to face in the office. Otherwise, we kept apart.

Freddy knew immediately, without being told, what had happened. "The look in your eyes gave it away."

"In mine, maybe," I sighed. "He never even looks at me now."

"He doesn't take his eyes off you!" protested Freddy. "He follows every move you make."

Was it possible? I began to watch Scott out of the corner of my eye. The minute I confronted his gaze, he turned away and pretended he hadn't been looking.

I relived each sentence, each gesture of our brief affair. What had I done to make him push me away? Had he meant it when he said "it was more than a fuck"? Were the hidden glances simple curiosity? Didn't he feel a burning sensation whenever we were in a room together?

History, I had learned from Al, was full of tragic, unrequited love affairs. And as Cindy reminded me, one-nighters. I explained it off to myself as a purely physical experience. A whole year of Al had not been as exciting as even a few minutes of Scott. But my experience with men was limited. Maybe there were hundreds out there like him. After a while the branding teethmarks on my back faded; my violent feelings for Scott Garrison did not.

Fortunately there wasn't much time to mull over it during office hours. Christmas was around the corner, and everyone wanted to go to Hawaii in the same two weeks. The agency was bedlam. Tiki Palms ran out of rooms early in November, and we were forced into blocking space at any Hawaiian claptrap that would accept our price.

It was so tight in Waikiki that even our competitors were calling us for rooms. They were, of course, refused. "We're not in business to help out other agents," said Nicole. "We have enough trouble with our own clients."

In the midst of this frantic Christmas rush, an atomic war was developing between our pretty receptionist and Helen Themis. I personally suspected Pretty Priscilla of deliberate, vengeful, premeditated sabotage. Freddy claimed, in her defense, that Priscilla was simply "a dumbshit of a secretary."

One morning, after receiving three unintelligible messages and a customer complaint of faulty ticketing, Helen stomped through the office screaming obscenities about the last five generations of Priscilla's grandmothers, marched into Mr. Gordon's office, and slammed the door.

"That motherfucking, cocksucking, painted whorina you got out there," we could all hear from behind the door, "doesn't have sense enough to pour piss out of a shoe with both ends cut off and the directions written on the heel."

Seconds later, Ralph Gordon was in the reception area with a teary-eyed Priscilla. (I had to admire her skill with makeup: not even a teeny smudge of mascara dripped down her cheeks.) "Mr. Gordon," she sniffed, "I just don't understand those *people*. I don't speak Greek."

"You can take a name and number, cantcha?"

yelled Helen. "Eh? That too difficult for your butterfly brain?"

Ralph looked from Helen's red-violet face to Priscilla's pink smudgeless tears. This was not a man trained to deal with the intricacies of an emotional crisis. He glanced helplessly around the room fishing for a solution. His eyes fell on me. "You," he said with finality.

"Me?"

"Learn Greek. Priscilla, whenever a call comes in for Helen and she's out, give it to Emily."

With that pronouncement, he fled the room.

Helen treated me to dinner that night at a customer's Greek restaurant. Three hours and many Ouzos later, I knew enough Greek to say, "Hello, Helen is not here. Do you want a ticket to Greece? Please give me your phone number. Helen will call you back." Delighted with my new proficiency, Helen offered me "a chance-of-a-lifetime business proposition." Remembering her former offer of a shipping magnate, I begged her to let me in on it. From the depths of her shoulder bag she produced a dog-eared black-and-white snapshot of a young man about nineteen years old.

"Eh?" She winked at me. "What do you think?"

"Helen, does he know the wet head is dead?"

"You could give him a shampoo once he got over here from Greece. Listen," she leaned toward me confidentially, "all you gotta do is marry him."

"*Marry* him! I'm not sure I even want to go out with him."

"For five thousand dollars?" She raised her eyebrows and nudged me. "Actually, you don't have to sleep with him. It's just 'til he clears Immigration."

"Helen, I—"

"Five thousand dollars and a round-trip ticket to Athens. First class."

I shook my head.

"Okay. I'll make it six thousand dollars. I don't make much off these deals, a couple tickets is all. But my customers all have relatives, see, so if I can do them a little favor here and there—tell you what, I'll throw in a cruise of the Greek Islands for a honeymoon."

"I appreciate your offer, Helen, but—"

She stuffed the photo back in her purse, shrugged her shoulders and poured me another drink. "Ya see, honey, it's not enough in my business just to *speak* Greek, I gotta give 'em extra personal service or they go somewheres else. Everybody's got the same fare to Athens. Now if I could offer a discount—"

I began to wonder about the Spanish-speaking market in Los Angeles. There were a lot of fat commissions to be made off South American tickets. And we could offer them lower than anyone else. I called Ed Rodriguez the next morning to discuss a plan. Together we went to see Ralph.

Ed's airline had the cheapest fares to South America. Not being a member of the International Air Transport Association meant they weren't subject to any minimum tariffs. And unlike Pan Am, they had only three airplanes to maintain: one retired Electrajet and two back-up props. The voyage from Mexico City to South America left at three AM once a week if the weather was clear and the plane in good repair. It wasn't a bad deal, if you had the stamina and courage of a bullfighter.

Still, I felt the reason more people didn't take advantage of it was lack of advertising. Ralph agreed. Since I spoke Spanish, I was put in charge of the bookings. Within a few weeks of our first ad, we filled an entire Electra jet to South America. Apparently a lot of South American bullfighters wanted to go home for Christmas.

It was the day Rosita Wong, a Chinese Chilean, stopped by to pick up her ticket to Santiago that I had another inspiration. Rosita saw our brochures on Hawaii and became ecstatic. "I have some relatives there, too," she said. "Maybe next year I come back here and buy tickets to Hawaii."

Later Ralph ran ads in the Spanish newspapers for his Hawaii package, and to my amazement, these also sold wildly.

"Why do you suppose someone would come clear across town to buy a tour when there are so many travel agents in East LA?" I asked Ralph.

"Why does anyone come to us?" he asked me back. True, they did save a bundle.

It was the week before Christmas, when we were at the height of our madness, that I got a call from Cindy. "Bob's decided to take me to Hawaii for a couple of weeks and I thought I'd give you the commission as well as anyone else."

"Thanks, Cindy, but I really don't think our tours are—" I found it hard to imagine Cindy going from Bel Air to the Tiki Palms, even if there were a room available.

"We've got it all figured out," she said. "All you have to do is book it. We want to leave on the morning of the twenty-third and spend the night in Honolulu at the Kahala Hilton. Waikiki's become so tacky, we'd rather be out of town a ways. Next morning we want to leave for—"

"Cindy, in the first place, we rarely book the outer islands here, and in the second place, it's a week before Christmas. Hawaii's booked solid. You might be able to get on some deluxe package tour—"

"Bob and I aren't exactly the package-tour set, and we always fly first class." I put her on hold as I saw Scott coming out of his office.

"Scott, how would you like a fancy-ass rich client? I've got a live one on the line, and I don't have time to fool with her."

He picked up the phone in his office and emerged a few moments later. "I got her two weeks at the Mauna Kea. One of my customers canceled. She'll be here in a little while to pick up the tickets. She says she's having lunch with you."

"She is?" I hadn't taken lunch in weeks.

"Thanks for the business," he said warmly. "It was kind of you to think of me." Think of him? Every spare moment I had was filled with unseemly thoughts of the bastard. I glared at him and picked up another phone call.

Something within me snapped when I saw Cindy coolly walk through the door, hair just done at

Elizabeth Arden, in a smart, hand-tailored Mathew's pantsuit. I was worn to a frazzle, every hair out of place, phones ringing, customers flying in and out in every language.

I introduced her to Scott and felt the sharp daggers of jealousy as they walked into his office and closed the door. Life was unfair. Cruel. My meanness welled up inside me so badly that I turned to Freddy. "Why don't you join us for lunch, Freddy? Do you good to get out awhile." The least I could do to make me feel better was to spoil her lunch.

"I thought I'd join you, too," said Scott with a smile as he led Cindy out of his office. "That is, if you don't mind."

"Oh, no," I smiled. "Freddy's also coming."

Cindy shot a tiny dart at me, which lightened my spirits. *That cunt,* I thought of my cousin Cindy. She may have steak at home, but she'd sure like to sink her teeth into my Tarzan. To what ghastly extremes jealousy will drive our thoughts.

That lunch might have been the most miserable of my life. Freddy, on whom I was depending to fly into some obscene gay routine about cocks and assholes, sat mute, ordering dry Martinis. On the other side of the table, Scott and Cindy seemed to have an unending supply of subject matter with which to amuse themselves.

"He's quite charming," confided Cindy on the phone that night, "and that fag is very nice, too. At least he keeps his mouth shut."

What could I say? I wished her a happy trip.

15

The night before Christmas we were all on the verge of a sanity breakdown. When the last ticket had been written, Ralph shocked us by breaking out a bottle of champagne. Jim Johnson, the National Airlines sales representative, dropped in with a bottle of Chivas Regal. It called for a party, or as close to a party as Royal Beverly will ever see.

Jim Johnson was a young, handsome, likable type—if you liked dark suits, white shirts, and wing-tipped smiles. Nicole amused herself on occasion by flirting with him. "It's good for the ego," she claimed, "to know you can still attract a man ten years your junior." This afternoon she was more absorbed in Mr. MacCallister, who had stopped by with a present for her from Tiffany's, an exquisite pair of jade earrings. Priscilla, seeing the way clear for the first time, quickly moved in on Jim Johnson.

I had a few glasses of scotch with Freddy and Helen and tried not to look at Scott, who was across the room talking to Ralph. It became too much for me. I forced down a huge gulp of scotch and crossed the room.

He and Ralph greeted me casually and continued on with their discussion of charter flights. I tried to think of something intelligent to add when suddenly

Freddy, dear Freddy, called Ralph away. Scott and I faced each other.

I clutched my drink tightly, so he wouldn't see my hands shaking. "How've you been?" he asked pleasantly. I had just enough liquor in my system to be impatient with banalities. Scott sensed it and looked about the room for an emergency exit.

"I want to say what's on my mind," I blurted out.

"Go ahead," he said quietly. "What's on your mind?"

I knew my face was flushed. "Every time I see you—want to talk to you—I don't understand it. You push me away. Do you dislike me so much?"

His dark blue eyes reflected my sadness for a moment. "No, I don't dislike you." We stared openly at each other. Whatever his reason, I understood that it had nothing to do with his desire for me; that was still vibrantly alive. I reached out to touch his hand, but he backed away. Before I could say anything, he turned and walked over to join Ralph and Freddy.

I clenched my teeth to hold back the anger and tears. Was I nothing more than a transitory hole for him to deposit his feline sperm and cruelty? I couldn't let him see my pain. I'd show him he meant as little to me.

Inspiration. I desperately needed inspiration. Ralph Gordon? No, Ralph wouldn't understand a pass if it grabbed him by the nuts. Scott would never take Freddy seriously. MacCallister? Now there was a man to contend with. Winning Nicole's lover would impress Scott. But I'd have to compete with Nicole, and that was out of my league. I hadn't even rated a second night with Scott, much less jade earrings from Tiffany and Co.

I looked up. The solution stood staring at me from across the room. Sorry, Priscilla, but I need Jim Johnson now more than you do. She didn't stand a chance, in spite of her mascara that didn't run and pink fingernails that don't chip on type-writer keys. I had resolve.

And I had Jim Johnson wrapped up neatly like a Christmas package in minutes. Priscilla's seething glare assured me all my tickets would be filled in wrong for the next few weeks, but I was more interested in Scott's reaction.

He was oblivious to my conquest. I marched out the door on Jim Johnson's arm, defeated.

It occurred to me, just outside the door, that I had made several flirtatious promises to this stranger I never intended to keep. He pulled me toward him in the elevator and gave me a long, wet kiss. What did it matter anyway?

I sat naked, studying myself in the mirror, after Jim Johnson left that night.

What had I done?

It was one thing to go to bed with a man one loved and planned to marry (Al), and another, though equally valid, to screw when one felt a passionate attraction (Scott), but to fuck one man to get even with another? This was a breach of morality.

Besides, it didn't work.

Jim Johnson may be just another pretty face, but he didn't deserve such sleazy motives. Our hour in the sack had been uneventful, but I was willing to take the blame. Soon after New Year's, I gave him another chance at satisfying me. He was actually no better or worse than Al had been—the kind who climbs on board and humps with all his might until it's out. I wondered if the bridge between Jim Johnson and Scott might be spanned by Technique. I made up my mind to ask Freddy's advice over lunch the next day.

"How do you get a guy to eat you, Freddy?"

"Why don't you say it a little louder so the folks at the next table can hear you?"

"Freddy, I'm serious. This is important."

"Just shove it in his face."

"Oh, Freddy, you're no help at all."

"Look, I tell you what: next time he's over, give me a call. I'll fuck him while he's fucking you."

"How's that going to get him to eat me?"

He shrugged his shoulders, "Hell, at least it might be fun."

"Sure, for you." I pondered his last statement for a moment. "Why would you want to fuck someone who was fucking someone else? I mean, why wouldn't you want to fuck someone directly. Eliminate the middleman all together."

"Because you'd get hung up on me."

"Egotist."

"You would."

"What if you got hung up on me?" I countered.

"I wouldn't."

"How could you be so sure?"

"I don't fall in love."

"Never?"

"No. I lead people to think I'm in love. I play the role, feign jealousy, act possessive. I think up tender little surprises for my 'beloved.' My first patron was very rich—retail shoe outlets, hundreds of them all across the country. He kept me in his Beverly Hills mansion for five years, convinced he was the only man I ever loved."

"What happened? Did he get wise?"

Freddy laughed. "It was one of my tender little surprises. I went down to Royal Beverly, his travel agency, and picked up a one-way ticket to Hawaii. I stayed three months, hustled tourists, cultivated a sensational tan, then, when I ran out of money, I called my patron and asked him to send me a ticket home.

"Cashed that in and stayed another month. Finally, he lost his patience and flew over to fetch me. I was all right for a few months, then winter set in. I got antsy and charged a ticket to Acapulco. An Italian countess picked me up off the beach for the Welsh poet she was keeping. I lay around her villa for almost a year. It was wild. People like Merle Oberon dropping in. But eventually I got bored and wired my loving shoe baron. No answer. The countess paid the fare home. That was the worst time of my life," he added solemnly. "I had no money, my patron had found another lover— even gave him my XKE, the sonofabitch. I had to go to work."

"A fate worse than death."

"The only job I ever had was the Navy. Here I was, fast approaching thirty, and I didn't know how to do anything but hustle tourists. It was natural I should go to work for Ralph."

"I'm surprised he hired you after all he knew about your checkered past."

"Oh, he was firmly against it. Nicole put me to work one day when he was out of town. It was during the Christmas rush and one of the agents had just collapsed. Couldn't take it. Nicole called and told me if I could handle it, she'd convince Ralph to hire me. And that was it."

I talked to Nicole later about her hiring Freddy. "I don't regret it," she said. "He's been a good employee. I always liked him; there was something of the naughty puppy about his manner. The guy who was keeping him—you'd never know he was gay—not good-looking, but very masculine. He was quite smitten with Freddy, would have done anything for him. You know," she said thoughtfully, "I understand Freddy, his need to be loved and protected and secure."

"Yet when the security got too tight, he bolted."

Nicole smiled, "Don't we all?"

She gazed off for a moment, miles away, then returned. "Hey, how's your romance with National Airlines?"

I sighed.

"Lousy lay, eh?" She read me correctly. "I thought so. He's too good-looking. The handsome ones never learn anything unless a smart woman gets a hold of them."

"Can you really improve them?" I asked hopefully.

"Look, Emily, no man is a natural-born good

lover. He has to learn from someone. My present husband, for example—a gorgeous handsome man —he was so bad his first wife ran off with a lesbian."

"I didn't know you were married," I said incredulous. She had never before mentioned a current husband.

"Keep it under your hat," she laughed. "Ralph won't have a married woman working for him. He thinks married women have too much else to occupy themselves. Helen's an exception, but her old man's in the clinker."

Nicole went on to tell me that she'd been married for five years. I assumed it was the bank manager, though she didn't volunteer any information.

"Isn't Ralph hypocritical?" I asked. "After all, *he's* married."

"Ah, but he's a man, and according to Ralph, a man will always put his work before his marriage."

"That's a crock of shit."

"It's his ballgame; he makes up the rules. By the way, that National rep looks awfully married to me."

"How can you tell?" I asked her.

"There are signs. They never take you out on the weekend." Jim Johnson never had. "They always go home after sex." Jim Johnson always did. "And they have a certain guilty look around their eyes." I had never looked that closely.

"What's the best way to find out?"

"Ask him," she laughed. "You can tell if he's lying. It'll be written all over his face. I've never

understood why married men aren't more direct
with women. A lot of women like to go out with
them. I do."

"You do?"

"Sure," she laughed. "It gives us something in
common!"

But before I had a chance to pop the question
to Jim Johnson of National Airlines, I was whisked
away on the travel agent's wings of fate. I was on
board a flight to Hawaii.

16

Most travel agencies make their employees wait a year before they are allowed discount airline tickets. Strict IATA rules govern these trips and agents are careful not to abuse them. Ralph Gordon, as I noted before, made up his own rules. My first-class United Airlines ticket was made out in the name of Nicole Randall.

It was actually Nicole's idea that I make the trip after things slowed down in January. She felt an agent was better equipped to sell what she knew first-hand.

But my primary mission was not a familiarization tour. In a conference with Nicole and Ralph the day before I left, I was briefed on our Hawaiian organization, or, in this case, the lack of it. Christmas bookings never ran smoothly. There were too many people arriving and departing for there not to be errors. This season had broken all records for foul-ups, and the problem appeared to stem from our Honolulu representative, Luana Pinkerton. Ralph and Nicole wanted me to meet her and come up with a solution.

It made no difference whether this was a test of my ability or genuine confidence on their part. The thought of spending two weeks in Hawaii sent me into an orbit of delight, something Jim Johnson, with ten illustrated sex manuals under each arm, couldn't do.

I had cut off any contact with Scott. When he walked through the office I now averted *my* gaze. Though my attention was constantly pulled to wherever he was, ignoring him at least put me in control.

The afternoon before my trip he called me into his office and asked me to close the door. I stood before him, stiff and indifferent, gazing at the floor. If I looked at those dark blue eyes, there was a chance I'd melt into the rug and never be heard from again.

"I understand you're going to the islands," he began pleasantly.

I nodded and folded my arms awkwardly so he wouldn't see them shaking. "Anything you'd like me to do for you while I'm there?"

He got up from his desk and came slowly toward me, stalking his prey. "Yeah, I can think of a few things offhand." He smiled wickedly. "Perhaps I'll join you there. Would you like that?" It was a Cheshire cat grin. He was dangerously close. I had to strike or be clawed to death.

"No," I snapped, returning his gaze with an angry stare.

"You're a bad liar, Emily," he called after me as I flew out the door.

I wondered at the sudden change in Scott as I settled into my first-class United Airlines flight to Hawaii. The steward brought me little red booties, a Bloody Mary, and a set of earphones. I quickly plugged myself in, but turned the volume off. I needed time to think, and the plump elderly lady in the next seat looked suspiciously like one of our customers who'd like to chat for four and a half hours.

I had almost come to the conclusion that I didn't like Scott. Whatever his reasons, he had treated me very badly. Now he wanted to play again. The ball of yarn he'd ignored for months suddenly looked attractive. And how soon before he'd lose interest again?

I thought of that extraordinary night in San Francisco. The lower half of my body shook. How often in life does a girl have one of those nights? Perhaps it was wiser to grab up as much as you could. To hell with the consequences. Scott was more exciting than a hundred Jim Johnsons. And Scott Garrison in Hawaii—I only half-hoped he wouldn't come.

Champagne followed the Bloody Marys and a delicious lunch. It dawned on me that I was traveling, for the very first time, first-class. Don't let anyone tell you there isn't a difference, even when it's for free.

I floated off the plane in Honolulu, only to discover that there was no one to meet me. I hailed a taxi.

Coming off a first-class flight and announcing you're going to the Tiki Palms is a horrible adjustment. Taxi drivers are very class-conscious. With one look they can put you in your place faster than any bona fide socialite I've ever known.

Luana Pinkerton was at the main desk to greet me, full of apologies about my airport transfer. I was beginning to know how my customers felt when they were left stranded at the airport.

Dealing with the public over the telephone had made me acutely aware of voices—how some matched up with faces, while others seemed to have been thrown together by a madman with a weird sense of humor.

Luana Pinkerton's voice belonged to a Gauguin painting, a soft melody of white ginger blossoms and plumerias. The face and body belonged to the Wicked Witch of the West. She was the most disconcerting person I've ever met. Her long, narrow form was draped in a loud flower patterned muumuu, resplendent with ruffles and bows. Pink rouge was rubbed into crackling, yellow, thin cheeks, and steel-gray hair, frizzed up in a Forties-style permanent, about the angular, pointed face.

I was immediately invited to her suite for a drink, and though I would have much preferred to sack out for a few hours on Waikiki Beach, business was business. She mixed me her version of a Mai Tai and poured herself a tall glass of straight Scotch over ice. At the end of this first drink, she began to relax enough to let the muscle control go in her left eye. For the rest of the evening I never knew which eye was really watching me.

I would rather have spent the evening alone in my room, or even in my closet rather than to suffer through four hours of Luana, but she was anxious to talk about herself and our Hawaii operation. The more work I could get out of the way, the more time I could spend on the beach.

Luana's past had all the excitement and adventure of any ex-Pocatello, Idaho, schoolteacher who retired to Hawaii after her husband, an insurance salesman, died. "Wasn't it prophetic," she said enthusiastically, "that my mother, bless her heart, gave me a Hawaiian name? It's as though she knew, in some mysterious way when I was born, that I'd be coming to Hawaii to die."

"How in the world," I choked, "did you ever find yourself in the travel business?"

"I've always been an active person," she assured me. "Lots of get-up and go. I said to myself, 'Luana, just because your life's partner has departed is no reason you should give up living.' Somehow I just slipped into this job, first as the bookkeeper, then eventually into managing the hotel. Of course, it's really your wonderful boss, Mr. Gordon, who keeps us on the map. You're so fortunate to be working for such a kind, generous man."

How generous he was, I didn't realize until the next morning when I began to go over her books. It wasn't easy to get her to part with them. At first, they were at the "bookkeeper's," but when I asked her for the bookkeeper's address, she took a few hours, and produced them herself. The first thing that struck me was the number of hotel transfers that had been billed to Royal Beverly—which many of our customers, like me, never received. I got hold of the man who provided the transfer service to and from the airport. He claimed that, aside from our regular group arrivals, he was often never notified of arriving passengers. Sometimes he'd drive all the way out to the airport and no one would be there.

Unfortunately, I had none of Ralph's own books with me, so I couldn't double-check our billing, but some of the customer's names I recognized. Many had cut their stays short and applied to us for refunds. Luana's bills to us didn't show this. I made Xerox copies of Luana's records for the months of November and December and packed them away.

It began to dawn on me that I would not be able to return to Los Angeles without an alternative hotel and tour service to present to Ralph. Luana may have been providing him with a cheap hotel, but it was, in the long run, expensive for him. Her mistakes, intentional or not, were eating away his profits.

I combed Waikiki for alternatives, talking with hotel managers, and collecting data. It wasn't easy to meet Ralph's price, but I found that the name Royal Beverly rang a bell with travel people in the islands. Doors opened readily for me, and I was treated, for all my twenty-one years, with respect.

In the meantime, I studied Luana's operation, comparing her booking and billing methods with other tour agents I was meeting, and made extensive notes.

It wasn't difficult to discover the reason for the Tiki Palms' thrifty operation. I had been in my room for three days, and the sheets had never been changed nor the bathroom cleaned. Sandy towels I'd dropped to the floor were simply shaken out and refolded. "You don't change your sheets and towels every day at home, do you?" Luana asked me when I mentioned it to her.

At night the noise from the two topless bars on each side of the hotel blared acid rock. It was impossible to sleep before two AM. Some of the "go-go" dancers rented rooms from Luana on a weekly basis, along with band members from the bars. It was a seedy-looking crowd that lounged around the pool during the day, sipping beer from cans. I thought of all the pink, scrubbed families I'd sent over to spend their hard-earned vacation money in this dump.

Strangely though, I'd never heard any reprimands from clients about either the hotel or Luana. I asked one of my customers, who was staying there, how she was enjoying her trip.

"It's been just delightful," beamed the elderly woman.

"You like the hotel?"

"Oh, yes. It's very nice. Such pretty plants and foliage. Of course, it's not one of the newer places, but we knew that before we came. We adore Luana; she's been so helpful to us, arranging our tours. Such personal service. And we're so close to everything. Why, each morning we go for a walk down Kalakaua Boulevard to the International Marketplace. It's so pretty here. I wonder why we never came before."

I thought of the International Marketplace, the white-legged tourists in matching muu-muus and aloha shirts, buying souvenir Diamond Head–embossed plastic ashtrays. These were the people who work their asses off fifty weeks a year for two weeks of tropical splendor, the Kodak Hula Show and Greyline Luaus. These were my clients. A shudder of class-consciousness came over me. What was the fine line that separated the upper middle from the lower middle? Who am I to put down Luana and the Tiki Palms? These are the people who built America. They were entitled to—

"Hey, baby, wanna fuck?" I felt a masculine hand on my shoulder and spun around, ready to clobber what I thought was the drummer from the band next door who'd been offering me warm beer for the past two days.

It was Scott.

"There you go with that dumb expression on your face," he laughed. "Come on, I'll take you for the plane ride I promised a couple of months ago."

17

Evidently I'd left all my pride in Los Angeles, for I was packed and ready to go in minutes. Since it was Friday, I figured a few days off for the weekend wouldn't infringe on Ralph Gordon's time.

"You ever been initiated into the Mile-High Club?" he asked as we pulled into the airport. We were in the area for small aircraft, heading toward a bright yellow Cessna.

"Mile-High Club?"

"Great initiation," he said, stepping agilely onto the wing.

I followed him, less agilely, into the cockpit. It was beginning to dawn on me why they named it that. "But who flies the plane while we—"

"Automatic pilot."

"How nice of him." I laughed nervously, surveying the complex instrument panel. The plane belonged to an old Air Force buddy of Scott's who lived in Honolulu.

"Are you scared?" he turned his blue eyes on me with a sly Cheshire Cat grin.

"No, are you?"

"Good, then let's get this mother up and put the fear of God in you."

Heavy gray clouds hung over the airfield. It took a few moments to get clearance to taxi down the runway. I've always enjoyed the takeoff in a jet, but in a small plane you really feel the dramatic thrust of being airborne. We climbed up through the thick, cotton white, Scott receiving instructions on the radio. Seeing him handle the controls, I had no fear of our dropping out of the sky. I did wonder, thinking of the traffic around the airport, if we might run headlong into another plane.

Scott turned to me. "Now you're going to witness something spectacular. You'll only see this in a small plane." The nose suddenly burst into the blue sky. We were riding the crests of clouds over the ocean, soaring up and down on an air-bound roller coaster.

He let me take the controls. I was amazed at how natural it felt; I was like a child discovering how to run. God must have wanted man to fly.

Sunlight reflected golden off the wings; the sky matched the color of Scott's eyes. We stared at each other hungrily. If there hadn't been a Mile-High Club initiation, I would have invented one. Scott reached over and released the lever that dropped my seat back. "This must be the wild blue yonder they talk about," I mumbled as he pulled my clothes off.

We were breathless and giddy from the altitude, naked and laughing. The airplane vibrated beneath us, and all around, wherever you looked, was sky. "Scott," I giggled, "this is the most bizarre thing I've ever done, aside from the clipper ship. What's next?"

"Some women," he laughed, "are never satisfied.

Next, we're going to do it in a bed, missionary-style."

He was on top of me, about to enter when I remembered with a gasp. "Scott, my love—"

"Mmmmmmmm?"

"What do you do with a Tampax a mile up in mid air?"

As though he'd done it a million times before, he pulled on the string and opened the small hatch in the window. We watched in total fascination as the tiny tampon flew past us at great speed, the little string waving behind it like a propelling tail.

"I wonder if it will land on anyone?"

"Probably some poor bastard fisherman down there," laughed Scott.

"And now he's going to know God is a woman."

I was soaring upward, in absolute control of infinity. "Scott, we're breaking an altitude record. We're going to land on the moon."

"Watch your legs," he warned; they were dangerously close to the controls. "Or we'll land in the fucking Pacific Ocean."

"What a crash investigation!" I thought of my poor father with his evening paper.

Making love to Scott was softer here above the clouds. The savage intensity of the sea evaporated into a fine, powder blue mist. "There's a feeling like this," he told me, "during early morning maneuvers. You're all alone behind the powerful deafening engine of a fighter jet. You climb higher and higher until the sky just beyond turns black. You've touched the edge of the universe."

When Scott finally took over from the gracious

automatic pilot, we were making an arc over the turquoise sea. The sun was setting in a blaze of vermillion and scarlet. We struggled to pull on our clothes in the tiny cockpit.

"Pick an island, any island," said Scott.

"England."

"Smart ass. I'll drop you off at the Molokai Leper Colony. How does Maui sound to you?"

"Fantastic."

"Good. Because that's where I made reservations."

"Cocky sonofabitch. You didn't think for a minute I wouldn't go with you! What if I had gone ahead and made other plans for the weekend?"

"You'd have broken them." He was right.

We registered as Mr. and Mrs. Scott Garrison at the Royal Lahaina, an older luxury hotel with all the grace and charm of Polynesia. Our suite was on the ground floor with a private lanai facing the pool. Just beyond was the ocean.

Hawaiian music, which only that morning seemed hopelessly corny, now filled the air with romance. I looked at Scott's handsome face and wanted to pinch myself. Surely, this was only a dream.

After a swim, we changed for dinner and watched the hotel hula show. Maui's version of Don Ho sang "I'll Remember You." Scott and I grasped hands tightly and kissed. How many tourists mistook us for honeymooners?

"You ever had a really good massage?" he asked as we walked arm in arm back to our room that night.

"I've had a backrub or two in my time."

"That's like comparing Paris to Tijuana. I'm talking about a real massage. I used to have a girlfriend who was a physical therapist. She taught me some amazing things about the human body."

"I didn't think there was anything you didn't know."

We undressed and I lay on the bed; he sat astride me. It would have been tempting just to begin making love, but Scott wouldn't be hurried. With his long fingers he began probing my back and rubbing muscles that, until that moment, I was unaware I had. Nothing escaped him. In a slow, methodical rhythm, his hands explored and caressed my entire body. "People think there are only certain erogenous zones," he said, "but your whole body is erogenous." He began to lick a place on my back. Electricity flowed from it and covered me. "You see," he whispered, "that's every bit as sensitive as your clitoris." Then he went on to prove himself wrong.

I conjured up all I could remember of Freddy's lessons and began to improvise on my own. A low sound of pleasure vibrated in his chest. "You wonderful cat!"

"Tell me what you like," he said when we had stopped for a moment to rest.

"I like it all."

"That's a cop-out," he protested. "Tell me what would please you."

"I think I'd like to—go down on your nose," I laughed and began licking the end of his lovely straight nose. He squirmed away, then asked me again, this time seriously, "Why won't you tell me what you like?"

I thought of the terrifying passionate moment he had grabbed the back of my neck in his teeth like a cat. A rush of desire passed over me. But I realized if I told him to do that, it wouldn't be the same. "I don't like to plan ahead," I told him. "I'd rather things just happened."

"That's the most shallow thing you've ever said," he said, disgusted. How could one man be so loving and so cruel all in the same bed?

"I didn't mean to be shallow or evasive, Scott. I've never been this uninhibited with any man. Goddamn, if I get a sudden uncontrollable craving to suck on your big toe, I don't want to feel confined because it's not listed in the program."

"All right," he said softly, then smiled. "Go ahead, suck on my big toe."

"No," I moved my lips down his chest. "I made other plans."

"Where'd you learn to do that?"

"You like it?"

"Yes. I'm going to see that you're nominated for Miss Blowjob of Beverly Hills."

"Freddy taught me."

"You're full of shit."

A velvet-soft ribbon of sunlight caressed our shoulders as we fell asleep in the early dawn.

It was past noon when Scott's smile penetrated my dream. I opened my eyes to make sure it was really him, and not just the beautiful face I could only imagine before. We looked at each other for a long time, smiling, speaking with our eyes. Somehow I knew that whatever happened to us for the rest of our lives, we could always look back on this moment. Wordsworth may have had his hill of daffodils to recall in dark moments. I would have Scott's smile.

After brunch, we found a secluded spot on the beach and baked our bodies in the damp tropical sun.

"Tell me about your physical therapist. Did you love her?"

"No, I just used her."

"Then tell me about the women you loved."

"It would take too long."

"You're so mysterious. Tell me about your mother, then."

"Best blowjob I ever had."

I threw sand on him. "I'm trying to be serious, you asshole. Whenever I get personal, you shut the door and lock me out."

"All right. What do you want to know about me. I'll tell you anything."

"What were you like as a little boy?"

He thought a moment. "Pretty much like I am now."

"Sexy?"

He nodded. "And naughty. I used to put worms in my governess' bed."

"My God, what'd she do?"

"Quit. What would you do?"

"A governess. You must have been very rich."

"Very."

"Were you an only child?"

"I would have liked brothers and sisters," he said

wistfully. For the first time I felt I might be touching something. "But my mother was tiny, a delicate woman. Having me nearly killed her. She died when I was ten."

"Of what?"

"They never told me. One morning she went into her room and locked it from the inside. I cried and banged on the door. She kept telling me not to worry—that she was all right. But I knew I'd never see her again."

"You think it was suicide?"

He shrugged, "I don't know."

"What was she like?"

"Distant. She didn't like to be touched. But there was an air of whimsical beauty, like a princess from a fairy tale, and about as accessible. She had very large brown eyes—a little like yours." He studied my eyes for a moment, then laughed. "No. Her eyes were doelike, timid and frightened. Yours are—" He searched for the word.

"Wanton?"

"Yes. And I've never seen you afraid."

"Why was she frightened?"

He shook his head. "My father treated her like a precious piece of Dresden china. She played the piano—I remember sitting next to her—she had long white fingers that barely touched the keyboard. Chopin mostly. Off the music room was her rose garden. She adored roses; had them all over the house. My father collected Greek sculpture for the garden, just to keep her roses company. It was an enchanted place to play—Chopin intermingling with the fragrance of roses, the cold, shimmering marble statues. He sold the house after she died, refused to buy another one."

"What does your father do for a living?"

Scott smiled, "Nothing."

"You support him?"

"No." He traced abstract patterns in the sand that became dollar signs. "It's old money, Emily, landed money. Like a couple of prime downtown city blocks of Philadelphia. Generations yet to come won't go through it."

"Scott?" I sat up and looked at him in disbelief. "Why do you break your ass every day for Ralph Gordon?"

"When have you ever seen me break my ass at that place?" he laughed. "Let's go for a swim." The casual way he sloughed off my question, I knew it was important. After making love that night, we lay naked on our private *lanai* and looked up at the stars. I thought about being on the edge of the universe and Scott not having to work for a living.

"Haven't you ever met anyone before who didn't *have* to work for a living?"

"I suppose it's terribly middle-class. Only the wives of my father's friends don't work. But of my aunts—they all work, only my mother married well enough that she doesn't have to. Even then, my father works six days a week, ten hours a day sometimes."

"Would he work if he didn't have to?"

"Of course. It's in his blood. But you, a blue-blood, why do you work?"

"It wasn't until after my first marriage broke up. Then, if only for my own sanity, I had to do something constructive with my life. I considered buying a roofing company or a chain of hamburger stands —but the travel business sounded more—romantic."

"Why'd you get a divorce?"

"Why'd I get married?" he laughed. "I was just out of college, bumming around Europe. She was a concert pianist, the most exquisite beauty I'd ever seen."

"Sounds Oedipal to me."

"You're probably right. But she was the first girl who ever really held me off. I followed her around Europe for three months trying to get into her pants. Said she was saving it for marriage. So I married her. We lived in Paris for a while. She did concerts and I frequented museums. Emily, did you know there are rooms in the Louvre packed with Greek statues they don't even have room to display?"

"I never got to the Louvre. Paris seemed too pretty and alive to waste my time lurking about musty old museums."

Scott looked at me oddly.

"I also found my wife bored me," he continued, "so I began playing around on the side. It wasn't really satisfying, but it was something to do."

"What did she do about it, or did she know?"

"There were scenes," he said sadly. "Not very pleasant. Things were said." He stopped himself and began again on a lighter note. "One day she told me she was in love with a violinist and wanted a divorce."

"Did she take on the violinist to get back at you?"

He looked at me playfully. "What a rotten motivation for taking up with someone."

"Are you insinuating—"

"Lucky Jim Johnson," he laughed.

"You bastard!"

"You're quite the seductive little hussy when you want to turn it on. You thought I didn't notice. Nothing you do escapes me."

"A mean rotten cocksucking—" As I struggled to get loose, he tightened his hold around me and interrupted my tirade with a kiss. We made love again, long into the night.

I never realized how pleasing the visual sight of a naked man could be until that weekend with Scott. He had long, well-muscled legs, strong shoulders. But my attention, as usual, was drawn to that beautiful long, white, appendage hanging between his legs. He caught me looking, and it pleased him. "Like it, do you?"

"It's all right," I yawned, "but can you do any tricks with it?"

He looked down and scratched his balls. "I can make it spit."

"Do you have a name for it?"

"No, why?"

"I'm conducting a survey. Nine out of ten men have names for their penises."

"How about if I call it Emily?"

"That's very touching. I've never had anything

named after me before. Not even a yacht. Wait'll I
tell Mom."

"Aren't you going to name anything for me?"

I thought a moment. "How about my left tit?"

"What's wrong with the right one?"

"Left one's bigger."

"I'll be damned," he admitted after some obser-
vation. "I'd never have hired you if I'd known that.
No, wait a minute, the left one just sags more.
You've named a saggy boob after me."

"You should talk with those saggy balls dangling
on your knees."

He looked in the mirror. "They are dropped
some, aren't they?" It never occurred to me that
men go through middle age fright. Scott hardly
seemed old enough to be called middle-aged, but
I did notice the slightest start of a roll about his
waist, a softness to his skin—or was it a loosening?

The closer we got to Sunday afternoon, and the
end of our weekend, the more sullen Scott became.
We rented a car and drove into Lahaina for lunch.
It was a history-lover's paradise, with a quaint
tinge of bawdy whaling port nostalgia about it.
But Scott's mood was falling rapidly, and even
Lahaina with all its historical charm couldn't lift it.

I tried telling him about Luana Pinkerton and
the Tiki Palms. He cut me off with a curt, "Save it
for Ralph. This is my weekend. I don't want to be
reminded of that place."

Much as I hated to admit it, I was anxious to get
back to work. Can one ever effectively shake off a
middle-class upbringing?

We boarded the small plane in silence and flew

back to Honolulu. I looked out over the ocean and tried to imagine the spot where our lovely bodies had collided in mid air. The elusive point would never be marked by a monument of any kind. Even the Tampax had probably been swallowed by a disgruntled shark who mistook it for a fish.

"Well, thanks for the nice time," I told him as he put me into a taxi at the Honolulu airport. I tried to remember what he looked like naked, his beautiful long, white cock, but my eyes were blurring. He reached to close the door when I jumped out of the taxi and grabbed his arm. "Why do you do this to me? Where did I screw up? What did I say to make you so—so hard?"

He snapped out of himself and looked at me for the first time that afternoon. It was a look of regret. He hugged me tightly. "It was a beautiful weekend, Emily, one of the best of my life. No shit."

"But then, why?"

Scott glanced at his watch and I noticed the impatient taxi driver hanging on every word. "There's something I should have told you. We'll talk when you get back to LA," said Scott and rushed off to catch his plane.

I climbed wearily back into the cab, contemplating the wonderful world of Luana Pinkerton to which I was about to return. I was angry, frustrated, helpless. "Why does he act that way?" I muttered to the taxi driver who was waiting for some direction.

"If you ask me, lady, the guy's married. Though I know it's none of my business."

"No, it isn't any of your business," I said angrily. "Take me to the Tiki Palms."

He shrugged his shoulders. "My kids don't listen to me either."

18

I worked frantically in Honolulu for the next few days, then took off for the outer islands. I wanted to bypass Maui, so as not to clutter my memory of it, but the holiday was over. I had work to do.

For those who still think, after reading this far, that a travel agent's life is all romance, I beg you to follow a travel agent on a tropical tourist island. Dog-eared notebook in hand, the hot, sweaty, muu-muu-clad agent tromps through twenty hotels in one day, listens to the same speech from twenty toothy, grinning hotel managers and turns down twenty dinner and drink invitations from the same. It wasn't until I got to Kona that I had any relief.

It came in the form of a six-foot captivating tropical wonder named Kimo. According to this primitive Tahitian god, he was part Japanese, part Hawaiian and part Jewish. (I'm not kidding, his last name was really Schwartz; I saw his driver's license.) It was an unbeatable combination.

Kimo was guiding a deluxe American Express Tour of Japanese businessmen, speaking to them fluently in their language. He showed me how a travel agent can live very high on the Big Island for free. We took turns, using either the American Express or Royal Beverly name in exchange for drinks and entertainment.

I surveyed Kimo's tall, muscular body that moved so effortlessly under his brown skin. White teeth sparkled in the moonlight when he laughed. I fought off my thoughts of Scott. Was I so far lost that I couldn't bear to make love with another man? What if Scott, as the taxi driver so rudely suggested, was married? He was probably in Los Angeles this very moment massaging some adoring wife into a frenzy of passion. Kimo moved his lips down my neck. I tried to push him away. How could I have another man so soon after Scott? Kimo was undoing the top to my bikini. But what if Scott cast me aside again? Kimo was caressing my breasts. Oh hell, where had love and fidelity led me with Al?

Like smooth, slippery dolphins, Kimo and I were dancing an underwater ballet, gliding, surfacing, splashing against the sheets of my Hilton Hotel–room bed.

I was exhausted as I boarded the plane in Hilo. Kimo had piled me high with plumeria and ginger leis, compliments of American Express. I sniffed them, looked out the window and sighed as the huge jumbo jet pulled out over the ocean. My thoughts were still with Scott. I knew now it was useless to try to forget him by bedding other men. I slipped into my first-class red booties, had another Bloody Mary, and settled back to watch the "in-flight entertainment." Hah! United, if you only knew.

19

I staggered into the office the next morning loaded down with leis, notebooks, and hotel brochures. Nicole, Helen, Priscilla and Freddy crowded around my desk to pick over the souvenirs and find out about the trip.

"What I wanna know—" began Helen with a wink.

"Of course," I laughed.

"Okay," said Freddy. "Begin at the beginning. How was he hung?"

"That, my dear, was not his best feature."

"Hawaiian, eh?" asked Helen, who seemed to know all about those things. I nodded. "Yeah, that's why I go to Greece every year. Those Orientals, gotta stick a finger up their ass, holler snake, and hope you find it."

Scott walked through the door carrying a package. My heart jumped up to my throat. There it was, the guilt. How could I have ever been remotely interested in Kimo? As he came toward us, I imagined him stripped of his business suit. He must have seen me the same way. We smiled. It was our secret. He handed me the package. "Something just arrived for you from Hawaii."

"Aha!" said Helen. "Your Hawaiian lover!"

Scott threw me a question mark. "A Hawaiian

lover, Miss Emily?" he said sarcastically. "I thought this was a business trip."

"Probably sent you a tiny dildo carved out of monkey pod to remember him by," offered Freddy.

I tried to yank out the foot lodged in my mouth while the others urged me to open the package. If Kimo had sent me a present, Scott would know for sure I'd had another lover. I felt sick.

Inside the box was a six-inch-high plastic tiki god, with the Tiki Palms Hotel crest emblazened on its belly. There was a note from Luana Pinkerton. "We sure enjoyed your visit. Come back soon. Love, Luana."

I spent the afternoon in conference with Ralph and Nicole. They were curious to hear everything I had to say about the islands, in particular about Luana.

"So it would be your recommendation," concluded Ralph, "that we go with another hotel?"

"Not necessarily," I said. "Our customers are happy enough with her and the hotel. We've just got to get her unmuddled so you stop losing money."

Ralph Gordon rarely expressed emotion, but the idea of losing money altered his pale skin to scarlet. "How do I stop losing money?" he asked quickly.

"We devise a system that will plug up the leaks and keep her honest."

"Jesus Christ couldn't keep her honest," interjected Nicole.

"When the bills come in," I continued, "who checks them out for accuracy?"

Ralph shook his head. "I just pay whatever she's got down there. Who has time to follow up every detail? You, Nicole and Freddy are too important in sales, Priscilla's too dumb to do anything but answer the phone and fill in tickets. I certainly don't have the time." Scott wasn't even mentioned. It was obvious he had nothing to do with Ralph's operation.

"But that's just it, Ralph," I argued. "We give the customer a voucher for ten nights. He leaves after six for the outer islands and applies to us for a refund. We give him his money back while Luana sends us our voucher and bills us for the full *ten* nights. We give the customer a voucher for an airport transfer. Luana conveniently forgets to call the man to pick up the customer. The poor people are stuck waiting for transportation at the airport. Luana bills us for the transfer anyway."

"She's also making money off the tours she sells our people," added Nicole. "She should at least be splitting those commissions with us."

"Nah," said Ralph with an impatient wave of his hand. "It's like splitting hairs. What's she make on a Circle Island Tour? Eighty cents? How'd we even keep track of it?"

"I agree with Nicole. Why not issue the voucher here? It's easy enough to sell. Gray Line would honor our vouchers. I spoke to the tour manager over there."

Ralph shrugged his shoulders. "What about the transfers?"

"I also talked to the man who provides the service. We could contact him directly."

"More paperwork," Ralph shook his head. "We have to have just one person over there to deal with. If it's not Luana, it's someone else."

"Then we don't pay her for any transfers unless she gives us back the voucher. Right now she bills us whether they received it or not."

It was decided I would go over all Luana's bills for the last several months, double-checking with our refund files. In less than half a day I netted Ralph two hundred dollars. It wasn't long before he was also giving me the airline tickets to tally each month. Math had never been a strong subject in school, but then they only dealt in theorems and X's and Y's. Put dollar signs in front of numbers and they take on some meaning, I found. Bookkeeping was not nearly as fun as selling, nor in Ralph's opinion, as important. He had built his business on a sales foundation.

Scott was gone all day and left no messages for me. I went home and sat by my phone, hoping it would ring. Suddenly the little business triumphs of the day seemed slight. I'd have gladly burned all Luana Pinkerton's lousy bills for one phone call from Scott.

I realized I'd probably blown it all to smithereens by my own big mouth. I could always claim that the "Hawaiian" was just a cover for us, to throw the office some juicy tidbits. But how could I make any claims when he didn't call?

He strolled into the office the next day around noon, said a few words to Nicole, then left again without even acknowledging my presence. My internal organs twisted into terrible knots.

Cindy invited me over for dinner, since Bob was out of town on one of his usual business jaunts. I wasn't really in the mood, but another agonizing night by a mute telephone would end my promising travel agency career in a mental hospital.

"Isn't that the pits?" she consoled me when I arrived. She was trying to talk little Bobby into taking a bath. He was screaming and throwing his rubber Disneyesque bath toys at her. "Now, Bobby," she said soothingly, "let's show Aunt Emily what a good boy you are and climb into your bath." He raised the pitch of his screaming a few decibels and gave me a scorching look. Obviously, he was not interested in impressing me.

She picked him up bodily, arms and legs swinging—it would have been easier to pick up a porcupine—and sat him down amidst the rubber toys. He banged his little head against the glass shower door until she lifted him out again.

"If you're not nice," she said, smiling a June Allyson smile, "Aunt Emily's going to think all children are like this and she's never going to want to get married and have children." He responded with a swift punch on her nose, and he shot me another dirty look.

"I don' wanna take a bath! I don' wanna!" he screamed.

She looked at me apologetically. "He gets like this when Bob goes out of town. They're very attached. Now, Bobby," she said calmly to him, "if you don't want to take a bath, Mommy's not going to force you." She turned back to me. "It's not good to force them into things. Here, will you stay with him a minute while I go get a fresh towel?"

I looked helplessly at the screeching little monkey in front of me. He watched me carefully out of the corner of his eye. I decided to try a little child psychology of my own. Grabbing his shoulders tightly, I said in a low, menacing voice, "Now you get your little body into that bathtub, and enjoy it, or I'm going to break your precious little neck."

"Well, what do you know?" laughed Cindy on returning. "See, what'd I tell you? Leave them alone and they take the initiative to do things on their own. Are you having fun with your yellow ducky?" She splashed him gently. He looked up at me, then back at his Mommy.

"Ducky," he giggled and threw some water in her face.

"Kids," she sighed, in that way only mothers can do.

"What do you think I should do about Scott?" I asked her after we'd put Bobby to bed for the fifth time.

"Is he really worth it?" she asked.

"Worth it? We're talking about a maestro who orchestrates multiple orgasmic concertos on my body all night long. I've never had anything like it in my life!"

"My husband does that. A lot of men do. You just haven't been around enough."

"Oh." I tried to build him up by telling her about the Airplane Fuck. That was no small feat, but Cindy'd been around.

"I was going out for a while with the president of the insurance company where I worked. He took me up in the company jet—it even had a bed and a real pilot. I came over Bakersfield on the way back from San Francisco one night."

"Goddamn it, Cindy! You don't have to top everything I tell you." I was getting pissed off. There's nothing worse that being told there's nothing unusual about getting laid a mile up in midair.

Bobby was calling her from his bedroom and she ignored him for the first time that night. "Well, you think you're so fucking unique, Emily."

"I *am* unique."

"Oh, hell," she apologized. "I'm just feeling hostile tonight. Bobby's being a little monster, and Bob—he's gone so much of the time. It's been ten days now and he's only called twice. I thought I might hear from him tonight."

"They never should have invented telephones."

"This is such a big house," she continued sadly. "The maid doesn't speak English."

"Why don't you go back to work?"

"No. I don't believe in that. I think if you're going to have kids you should stay home and be a full-time mother to them."

"What about all the women who *have* to go to work?"

"All right. They *have* to go to work. I don't. I haven't any excuse. Besides, I'm tired of working."

"What about going back to school for a mas-

ter's, or volunteer work? You could take up needle-
point, or take on a lover."

"Emily! Is that all you think about? Sex? Wait
'til you get married. It's not always on your mind.
You'll see."

It occurred to me that I had come over there that
night to find solace and sympathy for my own
problems. I was getting involved in Cindy's, and it
depressed me even more. I went home and sat by
my own phone. Which didn't ring.

I wasn't in my office more than five minutes the
next morning when Priscilla buzzed me. It was
Scott. "Hey, Hula Hattie, meet me at the Luau at
noon. I'll buy you a welcome home Mai Tai."

We had a long "Welcome Home" kiss at the bar
and an even longer hug. I was afraid if I let him
go, he might evaporate. "I thought you'd forgotten
me."

"I've been in a snit all week," he said, by means
of explanation, not apology.

"What's the matter?" I would be loving and
understanding. I thought of Cindy and her porcupine.

"None of your business," he said, turning toward
the bar to get the bartender's attention.

*Well, now's as good a time as any to drop the
bomb,* I reflected. His moods were getting to me,
and I was seething with rage.

"Are you married, Scott?"

"You having a Mai Tai?" He pretended not to
hear me.

"Are you married? Answer me."

"Let's get something straight." He glared fiercely

at me. "I don't like to be ordered to do anything. Especially answer questions I don't want to answer. Now do you want a Mai Tai, or don't you?"

"No."

"What do you want?"

"I want to get the fuck out of here," I managed through my teeth, and I walked out. I hoped he'd come after me, but he didn't.

The travel-agency business allows you very little time to brood over troubles. When I stomped back into the office, I found myself surrounded by a hundred hairy, unwashed, belligerent flower children trying to buy charter-flight tickets to Europe. Nicole took me aside and showed me the source of our new misery. A full-page ad had been placed in the UCLA *Daily Bruin*. The fares round-trip were less than the round trip to New York. "God bless Ralph Gordon," muttered Freddy, flying past us.

"Treat them like dirt," advised Nicole, "or they walk all over you." I was to collect a hundred-dollar nonrefundable deposit and get them to sign a fine-printed paper.

"I'm not signing anything until I read it," said one irate law student, waving the paper at Nicole.

"It says we can cut off your leg and you can't sue us for it," said Nicole.

"What kind of an airplane is it?" asked a chubby, freckle-faced girl in torn jeans.

"A jet."

"What kind of a jet."

"A jet."

"I wanna know what kind of a jet."

"Do you want the flight or don't you? If not, don't waste my time. There are only so many seats in an airplane." How did I know Ralph filled six to seven jets? The girl turned and looked at the crush of students behind her, and plunked down her deposit.

Nicole's advice was sound. College students are taught to ask questions, to be cautious and intelligent consumers. They *know* about politicians and rip-off artists. But their desire to get to Europe cheaply during the summer overwhelms these finer instincts. As soon as pressure is applied, they snap like plywood. "Once you master the technique with these idiots," said Nicole, "they're the easiest of all to sell."

"What do you think is the real deciding factor?" I asked her.

Without hesitation Nicole replied with a laugh. "It's not their own hard-earned money they're spending. It's their parents'. Watch the same people come back here in five years for a trip to Hawaii on their own paycheck, and you'll see some people reading the fine print."

I staggered into my apartment that night, eased myself into a chair on the patio, and stared into space. Exhaustion had caught up with me. Hawaii, Scott, Cindy—and now the charter-flight students. I wasn't sure I had the energy to fix dinner, even with the gnawing in my stomach from having walked out on my lunch. There was a knock at the door. I pulled myself up. Had I gained a hundred pounds, a hundred years?

Scott was standing at the door, his tie askew, hair falling onto his forehead. He walked past me into the kitchen. "I need some coffee. I'm drunk," he announced and sat down under the harsh kitchen light. There were dark circles under his eyes, which now looked dull turquoise; deep lines crevassed around his mouth. I switched off the kitchen light and lit a candle. His features mellowed considerably. I made him a cup of instant coffee.

He sipped it and frowned. "You make the lousiest cup of instant coffee I ever tasted."

I picked up the china cup and smashed it against the far wall, then sat down at the table with him.

"That's what I like best about you," he laughed. "Your sense of humor." I wasn't even smiling.

The smile also left his face. He reached across the table and placed his hand over mine. "Yes," he said softly, "I am married. It's very complicated." His hand tightened. "Now don't ever run out on me again like you did this afternoon."

"Do you want to talk about her?"

"No. Suffice it to say she's a hell of a woman."

"Then why do you want to make love to someone else?" I said angrily.

"Not someone else. To you. And there are a lot of reasons."

"Give me one, and it better not be because your wife doesn't understand you."

He smiled sadly. "That would be a lie. She understands me very well. I want to make love to you, Emily, because—" He looked deeply into my eyes for a long moment, formulating his answer. "Because—I need you," he said simply.

I suddenly didn't want to hear any more on the subject, thinking if I ignored it, it might go away.

We made love quietly that night. He was still drunk, and I was too tired to be imaginative. I felt almost maternal toward him in his sadness, and found myself most unnaturally cradling his head in my arms.

"Do you have any children?" I asked him as we held each other afterwards.

"No."

"Do you want any?"

"You're on The Pill, aren't you?"

"I didn't mean with me," I snapped. "I meant— in general."

"I like kids," he said thoughtfully. "But I don't know what kind of a father I'd be."

"Probably like yours was."

"I had a dream about him once. He lived in an igloo in Alaska and I wanted to see him. There were miles of deep snow to cross. When I finally found his igloo, I had to crawl on my hands and knees through a narrow long tunnel. The walls of ice were transparent, so I could see my father sitting quietly in the living room, but he didn't see me struggling to reach him. He was oblivious to the cold; he didn't even know he was an Eskimo."

"Did you ever reach him?"

Scott rolled over on his back and looked at the ceiling. "No, I woke up before I got there."

I kissed the palms of his hands and closed my eyes. I thought of the little boy whose mother lived on a glass shelf of Dresden China, a father who inhabited an igloo, and a wife who—

I opened my eyes to see him putting on his clothes to go home.

20

"The difference between you and me is, you're hung up on the guy," said Freddy. "Love'll turn anyone into a blithering idiot."

"I am not in love."

"Well, whatever they're calling the disease these days, you break out in hives whenever he looks at another woman." Freddy had guessed, as had everyone else at the office that I was having an affair with Scott. We had almost ceased to be discreet.

"It's merely a strong physical attraction," I explained to Freddy, "and I am *not* hung up. I could leave him tomorrow."

"And not go through withdrawal?"

I nodded.

"My ass," he laughed.

Freddy and I were spending more time together, especially on the weekends. Since we were both involved with married men, we had a lot in common. "Now with mine," he continued, "I couldn't give a flying fuck if he left tomorrow, except that I'd miss my liberal expense account."

"Oh, come on, Freddy, don't you sometimes wish you could come out of the closet with the whole affair, go out in public and live with the man?"

"Are you crazy?"

147

"Well, I'm going bananas with all this secrecy and deception," I said. "It's not me."

"Then go back to National Airlines."

"Barf."

"I'd go crackers if my patron were hanging around all the time. I value my freedom more than honesty. Besides, if he were here all the time, when could I go to the Baths?"

"You could go together," I suggested.

"There are certain things, Emily, you will never understand."

The points Freddy made about freedom were lost on me at the moment. Scott, much as I hated to admit, was becoming the center of my tiny universe, and I was in agony to think I had to share him. Cindy, who had experience with married men, claimed I had it fairly good.

"Most married men wine and dine you until they finally get you to bed," she said. "Then all they want to do is stop by, have a drink of your liquor, and stick it in you. Psychologically, they can't handle the guilt. They're being naughty boys, and if Mommy catches them, they'll get their little fannies spanked.

"The only way to justify cheating on a wife is to do it with a whore. That isn't anything human. It doesn't take anything away from a good, clean wifey and mommy at home. If you don't happen to be a whore, they'll dehumanize you into a hole—a pleasant, if illicit jack-off, after which they jump into your shower, wash off the dirt, drop the towel on your bathroom floor and fly out the door."

"Yeah, the shower I sure can't understand," I

said. "If I ever get married and my husband climbs into bed smelling of soap, I'm going to know exactly where he's been. At least Scott still takes me out to dinner, sometimes to the movies. It's just that—he takes a damn shower and goes home!"

"You mean, he never has to excuse himself to make one of those ghastly furtive telephone calls?"

"Never."

"You sure he's really married?" she wanted to know. "Something's fishy. He's too out in the open."

"Maybe she trusts him," I suggested.

"Maybe she just doesn't give a shit is more like it," said Cindy. "Nobody's that trusting, especially a wife." I was unaware of the real reason for his openness.

Scott liked to keep track of dates—the historian in him. At the one-month anniversary of our Hawaiian Weekend, he decided on a commemorative celebration. We took Scott's plane to Las Vegas for the evening.

I borrowed a flashy sequined gown and fur from Cindy. Scott looked dashing in a white suit. Liz and Richard could not have looked more like movieland royalty.

I don't think I will ever feel entirely at ease in those glittering surroundings. The finer trappings of money don't bother me; watching people throw it away so casually and with such happy abandon was horrifying. An hour of sitting by Scott at a baccarat table had me shaking with disbelief. He dropped an easy five thousand dollars, shrugged his shoulders, and took me to dinner.

"You do this often?" I asked him.

"Once in a great while. You don't like it, do you?"

"You realize how long it takes me to earn what you just blew on that—that game?"

"Suppose I just gave it to you instead?"

"Then I'd feel like a whore."

"What's the difference of taking if from me or taking it from Ralph?"

"I'm working for Ralph."

"You'd make a lousy whore, anyway," he laughed.

"What's that supposed to mean?"

"You're too fucking independent."

"I'd think the independent ones would be the most successful financially. They wouldn't be giving up most of their hard-earned money to some pimp just for security."

"Do you ever stop thinking business?" sighed Scott.

"Well, sometimes." I smiled, reached under the tablecloth, and unzipped his pants.

"I'm surprised you haven't figured out a way to turn that into a profit."

"If you learned a few more tricks, I might be able to convince Ralph to let me run a guided tour by it, and—" He interrupted me with a kiss, and I felt him place something around my neck. It was a beautiful antique gold watch on a chain. My initials were engraved on the back.

"Scott, it's exquisite! It's the most beautiful present I've ever received from a man." Could I really count the album of "Bob Dylan's Greatest Hits" I received last year from Al? "But I didn't get you anything, Scott, I feel terrible."

"Time," he said like a historian, "is the most important thing you can give anyone. When it comes right down to it, that's all we have."

Flying home that night, I was a little tipsy and feeling good. We made love on a soft, starlit blanket of desert air. "Scott?" I suddenly wanted to know. "Do you enjoy the time you spend with your wife?"

He looked at me for a moment, then out into the night. "What do you want to hear?"

"The truth."

"She—it's very difficult for me, but yes, for the most part, I enjoy being with her." I hated his tone of voice. It was too tender. I longed to detect even an inkling of acidity. She was suddenly in the airplane with us, crowding me out into the sky without a parachute.

"If you enjoy her, why do you spend so much time with me?"

"When I was married the first time, it was nothing to go out, get drunk, and get laid every night with a different woman. It was meaningless, superficial."

"Oh, I see. Now you've cut back to only one mistress. It's like economizing on your morals. Minimizes the guilt."

"Emily—don't—" Moonlight was reflecting sparks from his eyes, which were now brooding dark. "I never meant to have you that night on the ship. I just wanted to go out of town, have a good time. I'll never forget how you looked that first day you came to apply for the job. So cocksure of yourself, those big impudent eyes, young tits poking out at me. And you were bright, undeniably bright."

"Is your wife intelligent?" I immediately regretted my question. The mere mention of her oppressed the desert air around us. "Don't answer that, Scott. I don't want to hear any more about her."

"Then don't ask me any more questions," he said simply.

"Does she know about me?" I couldn't help myself.

He turned his head and stared into the night. "Does it hurt her to have to share you?"

Scott looked back at me and saw the tears streaming from my eyes. He pulled me to him and I lay my head down on his lap. He stroked my hair softly while I cried.

21

I don't like to be reminded of the passage of time. Seconds and hours ticking by on my wrist have always annoyed me. The antique gold watch was a historian's gift, a cat proudly presenting the bloody mouse to his beloved mistress. I would wear it lovingly, but never wind it.

I wore it to work the next morning, ready to bask in the compliments I would receive when suddenly my insides fell out, splattering mercilessly onto the floor. I saw who awaited me in the reception room.

"Hello!" said Al. His large, white, smiling teeth looked grotesque under the long, fluffy beard. "Your mom told me you were working here. Said to tell you she sends her love and to write once in a while." He waited for me to laugh and when I didn't, he continued on. "Oh, Emily, I'd like you to meet Alice, my fiancée."

My mouth fell open. The painful love I'd felt for him—the hurt I'd been suppressing—began to boil up in me like angry venom. "What do you want?" I said, hanging icicles on every word.

The emaciated Alice had long, stringy hair matted under an Indian headband. She looked up at me through granny glasses, startled. Al went right on as though I'd just given him a hug and a

153

kiss. "We were interested in charter flights, for one thing."

"Priscilla here can take care of you," I said and headed toward the door. At that moment Ralph Gordon walked in. "Excuse me," said Al quickly to him, "but are you the owner of this agency?" Ralph nodded. Al extended a hand. "How do you do? I'm Al Girard, an old friend of Emily's, and I've got this great idea for a tour if you've got a few minutes."

"Sure," said Ralph. Like the singer who read every sheet of music that came his way, he never knew when he'd come up with a hit.

Ten minutes later, Ralph asked to see me in his office. "Your friend Al has an excellent idea for a UCLA extension course in Europe."

"Since when have you been at UCLA?" I asked him.

"Last semester. That's where I met Alice. We both had this course on the Middle Ages and that's where I came up with the idea."

"It just might work," said Ralph enthusiastically. "It's a—what did you call it?"

"A Hundred Years in Thirty Days," supplied Al. "We visit all the battle sights of the Hundred Years' War. It started in 1337 when Edward III sent a letter of defiance to Philip of Valois in France. Imagine, a hundred years of war. Blows your mind."

"I'm sure it does," said Ralph, cutting off any further discussion of the content of the tour. "You say we need a presentation, Mr. Girard?"

"No doubt about it," said Al with authority. His

bout with drugs had evidently done nothing to mar the fraternal, likable glibness I used to find so irresistibly charming. "I've already talked to the history department, and they approved. Only thing is, they require bids from at least two sources. I don't know how many agencies will bid on it. You'd have to know the period historically to plan a tour around it. We've got to work fast if we want to get it into their summer-extension mailing. But it's got to be the right kind of presentation."

Ralph turned to me. "Emily, I want you to work on this with your friend Al. Get the pricing and itinerary figured out along with the presentation."

"Wouldn't Freddy be better at this kind of thing? He's had so much more experience with large groups."

Ralph shook his head. "He's never been to Europe or college, and Al says the thing has to look like a term paper with footnotes and that kind of garbage. Al claims you write term papers better than anyone he knows."

I glared at Al, remembering all the term papers I'd written for him when he was too smashed to find his typewriter. "Mr. Gordon," I said as evenly as possible. "Having taken a few history courses, I must be honest. The Hundred Years' War, even for scholars, is a tiresome, dry subject. Al's a good friend of mine, but I don't think this tour will generate enough interest to get off the ground."

Ralph looked to Al for a rebuttal. "I disagree, Emily. *You're* not into history. Wow, you should have seen the turnout for our Middle Ages class. Over two hundred people! All we need is a super-dynamite presentation and we'll have people standing in line to go on the tour."

The rebuttal seemed to satisfy Ralph. And a presentation didn't mean he was out any money. "We'll try it out," he said.

"What are you doing tonight?" Al asked me. And before I could answer, he said, "I thought we could meet you here after work and get the thing done right away. Alice can type it up as we work." Ah, so he had found another willing writer-typist.

I looked at Ralph. What I did on his time was his business, but on my *own* time?

"I'll pay you overtime," Ralph assured me, reading my thoughts. "Oh, and as far as pricing the tour, figure a hundred dollars a head for Al and a hundred dollars for us."

"Is there any justice in this world?" I asked Nicole later. "I'd rather spend my evening in a crowded cage with a cobra than see that bastard again, especially see him make money with my help. And if the damn thing sells, Ralph'll probably put me in charge and I'll never get him out of my life."

"That's one of the problems in working for someone," she sighed. "You can't always do business with whom you please. How much money are you making now, Emily?"

I was up to $450 a month.

She laughed. "Now on this tour, your friend Al makes a hundred dollars and Ralph makes a hundred dollars. How much will you see of it for all your work and agony?"

"But most of his tours are so low-priced," I argued. "He's doing a lot of volume, but he's not clearing that much. Since I've been doing the books on his Hawaii operation, I've been amazed how little he makes. How does a travel agency that doesn't deal in volume even stay above water?"

"Ask Scott about that some time. He thought this business was a service to help rich people plan their vacations. I'll tell you the secret to making money in a travel agency," said Nicole. "You know all those nonrefundable deposits we collect—especially for the charter flights? Ralph has ten days or so before he has to pay off the airlines. You can double your money in ten days, or even sooner, if you've got enough ready cash to play the stock market."

"Double your money?" I wondered why anybody wasted their time with baccarat.

"How often do you read the *Wall Street Journal?*" She took a current copy out of her top desk drawer and handed it to me.

"I don't think I've ever read it in my life."

Nicole shook her head in dismay. "I'll never understand why mothers don't buy their daughters subscriptions to the *Wall Street Journal* instead of all those silly glamour magazines. It would stand them much better in life. My adopted mother used to quiz me on its contents every night before I went to bed."

"But what if one of the investments didn't pan out? What would Ralph do then?" I asked.

"He's got enough cash to cover it, but he's rarely wrong. Not all agents are that smart, especially in the charter business. That's why the nonsched airline business has such a bad name. I imagine one day they'll pass a law requiring agents to keep their deposit money in a trust account, just to stop that kind of abuse. In the meantime, Emily, you'd be wiser to have an affair with a stockbroker or a banker than with someone who can't even make a go of it in this business."

It was the first reference she'd ever made, no matter how oblique, to Scott. I wondered if her opinion of him would change if she knew how wealthy he was. Probably not. I couldn't see Nicole ever having any respect for a man who couldn't make it on his own.

22

"Why they insist on calling it the 'Dark Ages,' I'll never know," said Scott. "The fourteenth century was a fascinating period. Knighthood was in flower. Gothic architecture—you'll have to include all the great cathedrals in the tour. If I remember my history, the Hundred Years' War was a power struggle between the Plantagenets and the Valois."

"Maybe you should work on it," I said sarcastically. "It doesn't interest me in the least."

"That's because you're too emotionally wrought up over your ex-boyfriend."

"Scott, I hate to admit this to you, but what some English king tells some French king in 1337 intrigues me about as much as what Ralph says to his dog. Maybe less."

"Emily, your apathy is appalling," laughed Scott. I could see he didn't believe me. "What does intrigue you?"

"Your beautiful long, white cock," I whispered in his ear. He called the waiter over to pay the check. We were having dinner before I had to meet with Al.

"I wish there was some way I could get out of this tonight," I sighed. "I know I'm going to say or do something rash. I loathe him, Scott. Have you ever felt that way about anyone?"

"There's a thin line between love and hate," he reminded me.

"You could love Lee Harvey Oswald?"

"We're not talking about Lee Harvey, we're discussing a guy you were in love with and wanted to marry. The guy you gave your virginity to."

"You make it sound like it was a present."

"And you still feel something for the guy. A woman always remembers her first—"

"I don't still love him, if that's what you're getting at," I said vehemently. I suddenly wanted to scream at Scott that I loved *him*. Love, there it was snapping at my heels again. How could I admit it to Scott when I couldn't admit it to myself. Besides, etiquette dictated that the man declare his love first. Etiquette? Balls. I was just terrified that if I told him how I felt, he'd tell me it wasn't mutual.

"You can't keep licking your wounds," said Scott reasonably.

"Would you stop shoving platitudes down my throat? It makes my dinner hard to digest."

"All right," he laughed, "have a good go at him. Maybe that's what it will take to get him out of your system. Otherwise you're going to take out your resentment on every other man you know for the rest of your life."

"I've never taken anything out on you!" I protested.

"But you hold back. You're still afraid to let go."

"I am not! I'm not afraid of anything."

He leaned over and kissed me. "No, my sweet

darling, maybe not," he laughed. Sometimes I could see Scott as a total stranger. His physical beauty sent shivers down my spine. It seemed impossible to hope that this man could really care for me. As great as Cindy assured me his attentions were, they didn't seem enough. Only having him completely seemed enough, though Cindy warned me about issuing ultimatums.

"Nothing will make him drop you quicker," she had said ominously.

"But how do I get him to leave his wife?"

"One chance in a million he will," Cindy shook her head. "Men just don't leave wives easily, even when they're miserable. A wife is a known quantity. Something they can depend on. These guys sit in garbage cans all day and complain about the smell, but ask them, why they don't just climb out? Never occurred to them. You better face up to enjoying this affair for what it's worth."

What is it worth? I thought. A wire was slowly coiling around my heart. I knew sooner or later I'd have to make a choice. Either cut the wire, or let it strangle me.

23

*Al came to the office prepared with several text-*books, notes, and other people's term papers he'd taken out of the library. I supplied the rate books. Since this was the age of chivalry, I decided to make an effort at being civil. I wondered if the Plantagenets and the Valois had made as great an effort to avoid open warfare.

"I think it would be a gas to stay at all the colorful little local inns," began Al. "There are still towns where most of the major battles were fought."

"Al," I sighed, "colorful little local inns may be fine for you and Alice, but most Americans prefer bathrooms attached to their rooms. I think we better stick to major hotels in major cities. We can bus people out to the battle sites, and they can have their own hot shower when they get back each night."

To my amazement, he agreed.

Perhaps the evening would pass without a single drop of blood shed.

"We've got to decide right off which are the most important cities," I said.

Al consulted his notes. "London, Paris, of course, then Tours, Bordeaux, Poitiers."

I got out a map of Europe and we plotted a

reasonable itinerary. I checked hotel rates, European charter bus rates, air fares, figured in food costs for two meals a day. Within an hour we had the itinerary and tour cost. I was beginning to think I'd built a monster in my mind. Al was agreeable to everything.

Then we began work on the presentation. He was insufferable. Every few minutes he burst forth with some boring pronouncement from one of the textbooks, like:

Crimes are not committed by the enemies alone, some have seized men women and little children, without regard to age or sex . . . ravished wives and daughters and seized nursing mothers. . . .

"That was written way back in 1433!" He looked to Alice, who nodded with enthusiasm and approval.

"How meaningful," I said dryly. "Now let's figure out what the sights are in Bordeaux."

"You're missing the whole point of this tour, Emily," said Al. "We are taking these people on a tour of the longest war in history. A whole century of war! We study it: the causes, the effects— and maybe, just maybe we'll blow a few minds out, make them think about the futility of war. Look what we've done in Vietnam. We never learned from history!"

"And here, all along, I thought you were in this thing for the money," I said.

Alice was looking at me strangely.

"You never did understand me," said Al angrily. "We never could communicate."

"I guess I lack your sensitivity." My eyes were shooting daggers. "Al, it's ten o'clock and we're only as far as Bordeaux. Perhaps you have altruistic motives, but I'm in this for the money."

"You always were a fucking materialist, Emily."

"And you've always been a raging asshole."

Alice jumped to his defense. "Al happens to be a very sensitive, warm human being."

I was hot now, in the thick of battle. Chivalry was dead. I was out for blood.

"Wait 'til you get pregnant, Alice, watch how sensitive and loving—"

"For your information," she said coldly, "I am pregnant."

I was stunned for a moment. She was actually going to have his kid. Not that I'd wanted it, really, but—"You're lucky he gave you the choice. You sure it's yours this time, Al?"

"Emily," he said sternly. His cheeks were turning lavender under his beard. "It's all over now. Let's just forget what happened, okay?"

"Oh, sure, Al. It was easy enough for you to forget. It was easy for you to forget to give me any money, any moral support. It wasn't your body that was raped on the abortionist's table. It wasn't your body that had a child scraped out of it. It was easy for you to forget to call me afterwards to see if I was okay. You're a fine historian. As far as you're concerned, nothing happened, nothing at all. I wonder that ravished women are mentioned at all in history books written by men. It's so easy for them to forget us. Oh, he'll be a fine father to your child, Alice. You'll find him a tremendous comfort. Just don't forget to buy him a Father's Day card once a year so he doesn't forget he is one."

I was finished. My two adversaries lay bleeding on the floor, stripped of their armor.

"Let's go home, Al. Please, let's go home now," pleaded Alice weakly. He was looking at me, eyes filled with hatred. He couldn't let Alice see it.

"I'm sorry, Emily. It's probably too late, but I am sorry. You were always so laid back and practical about everything, even when I flipped out that time. I never thought something like an abortion would get you bent out of shape. When you didn't call me again, I just assumed it was cool."

I'm not a saint. I couldn't forgive him. Could the Plantagenets forgive the Valois? I suspected he staged the last speech to save face with Alice.

"Go on home," I said coldly. "I'll finish up the presentation." And with a final stab, I said, "One more of your little creations, Al, is nothing."

24

The office was very still after they left. I had never seen it so quiet. I stared at the papers and history books in front of me. Can people really learn from the past?

I thought about what Al had said. Maybe my flip, practical number had fooled him into thinking I had no feelings. Even with Scott, I was afraid to say how I really felt about him. Did I expect him to read my mind? Perhaps he was only waiting to hear me say I loved him before he declared himself. He had intimated as much at dinner. I resolved to let him know.

After another cup of coffee I sat down at the typewriter. Time passed quickly as I let myself flow into the old college prose style I'd left behind. I constructed my paragraphs carefully to prove a point, lifting colorful phrases here and there from European tour brochures and art history books.

What an odd sensation to witness dawn from a Beverly Hills office building. I looked out over Wilshire Boulevard, down toward the Miracle Mile. Perhaps I'd see the ghosts of the hulking dinosaurs who used to slosh up to Fairfax on a sunny morning for a drink, only to get stuck for all eternity in the La Brea Tar Pits. There must be a lesson in that, something one could base a religion on. But my head was stuffed with cotton and my fingers were numb from typing. I looked at the antique watch ticking patiently around my neck. Scott had wound it for me. It was six AM.

The front office door opened. Hadn't I locked it in my fury from the night before? My heart jumped to my throat. Perhaps it was an armed robber come to steal blank tickets. I could barricade myself in Scott's office, call the cops. I tried to hear what the robber was doing. No sound. He probably wore sneakers. Maybe I only thought I heard the door open. Anyone who saw dinosaurs sloshing—

I took a deep breath, a sip of coffee, and opened the reception room door. Sitting there quietly was a slight, red-headed girl in a rumpled yellow shirt and faded jeans. Her head was propped against the wall in an effort to keep awake. *One of our weird charter customers,* I surmised, *probably stoned.*

"Hi. Sorry. The office doesn't open for a few hours." She blinked and looked up at me.

"Oh, well, do you mind if I just stay here? I'm waiting for someone."

Now they were using our office as an alternate student union. "Waiting for whom?"

"Mrs. Randall."

I knew Nicole often came in early, but why would she tell a customer six AM? I returned to my desk, leaving her in the reception room. Another hour of work and I'd be done with a hundred years of war. It's a lot of battles to fight in one night.

I was on my way out when Nicole arrived. "You

want a charter flight?" she asked the girl coldly, in her charter-flight voice. The young customer shook her head and stared at Nicole, who looked at me for assistance.

"She's here to see you," I shrugged.

"You don't know me," said the girl finally in a faltering voice, "but—" I suddenly guessed why this girl had come. Nicole's pained expression told me she did too.

"Jeanne?" The girl nodded. "But how did you know I was—alive?"

"My stepmother told me after Dad died last month. I wanted to see you."

"But why didn't you write and tell me you were coming? I could have sent you a ticket."

"I just left suddenly. Hitchhiked. My stepmother and I had a fight."

"Does she know where you are?"

"I don't want her to know," said Jeanne bitterly. "I figured you'd understand that."

"Come on, honey, I'll take you home." Nicole held a tentative hand out to Jeanne, but they didn't touch.

I turned back toward the office. No sense going home. With Nicole gone for the day, it would be crazy. I had some breakfast at the coffee shop downstairs, combed my hair, and returned to work.

Ralph was reading over the term paper I'd left on his desk. "What the hell is this?" He shook the thick stack of papers. "I was just kidding about footnotes. It's ridiculous. They'll never read all this!" Ralph obviously had little appreciation for the finer points of scholarship.

"Historians are in love with footnotes, Mr. Gordon, believe me." I saw Scott heading toward his office, and I hailed him over. "Tell Mr. Gordon how historians feel about footnotes, Scott."

He backed me up. "History books are loaded with them, Ralph. Why, I've seen up to two-thirds of a page taken up by a single footnote."

"Wouldn't it be easier just be include the goddamn thing in the text? Think of printing costs."

"Ralph, you think like a businessman, not a historian."

"And I'm paying out my tax money to support these numbskulls at state universities?"

He thumbed through the presentation quickly. He had no intention of reading it. "So you think they'll buy this thing?" I shrugged. "I'll try anything once," he sighed.

I went into Scott's office and closed the door, bursting to tell him what had happened to Nicole.

"Her daughter?" he said, surprised. Nicole kept so secret about her life, I probably shouldn't have betrayed her confidence. Feeling guilty, I quickly changed the subject back to my evening with Al. "Tell me about it later, love," he said nearly out the door, "I've got some appointments and I'm already late."

"Poor Nicole," said Freddy over lunch that afternoon. My precautions with Scott had been unwarranted. Gossip spread through that office like melted butter on toast. "Same thing happened to me once," said Freddy.

"One of your kids showed up?"

"No, my mother."

"Where had she been?"

"Farting around, I guess. She up and left me one day in a high chair and that was the last I saw of her until a couple of years ago. She heard I was living well in Hollywood and figured to cash in on some filial affection."

"Of which I'm sure you had gobs. How come she left you?"

"She claims it was the old man. Who knows? She was such a lush by the time I saw her."

Scott returned late in the afternoon, angry and impatient. My usual ploy was to play gently around his erratic moods, ignoring them until they disappeared. But a night without sleep and the general trauma of the day and night had worn the soft edges off my personality. I thought it wiser to avoid Scott entirely, in his current state.

My plan failed. He was at my desk within minutes with a letter he wanted me to type.

"I'm really pressed for time, Scott," I tried sweetly. "Do you think Priscilla could handle it for you?"

"She's a lousy typist. I want you to do it."

I looked at the pile of my own unanswered correspondence. My head ached as though someone were drilling holes in each temple.

"Well, do you type it," he asked impatiently, "or shall I take it to Ralph?"

"I wasn't hired to be your goddamn secretary," I snapped. "Type it yourself." A few moments later,

I was regretting my rude behavior and went to his office to apologize.

"Scott, you'll have to understand. I was up all night with that wretched tour and—"

"Don't forget I hired you, you uppity little bitch," he interrupted angrily, "and while I'm the general manager here, you'll fucking well do what I tell you."

"Does that include the blowjobs, sir?" I asked sarcastically.

"Don't think I wouldn't see you fired." He glared at me.

I took the handwritten letter he'd wanted me to type, crumpled it in my fist, and dropped it on the floor. "I'll see that shoved up your fine ass before you fire me."

25

If Scott did want to can me, this was a bad time to convince Ralph of my incompetence. UCLA had enthusiastically bought the Hundred Years' Tour and was begging him for similar presentations of a marine biology tour of Hawaii and an anthropology tour of Mexico. Fortunately for me, these were all outside the history department.

Firing might have been an easier way to go. A cold frost that was impossible to penetrate had set in between Scott and me. I made a few attempts to apologize, but they were only met by an indifferent stare. If he were still angry at me, I might have been able to deal with it, but he completely excluded me from his thoughts. I watched, as I used to, out of the corner of my eye, to see if he were looking at me. He wasn't.

It took a few days for the shock to register. This was the end Cindy had predicted. It had been a bang, not a whimper; an abrupt, absurd finale. Intellectually, I accepted my fate, emotionally I refused.

Cindy tried to cheer me up. "You had a good affair, Emily, now move on. You had to find out for yourself about married men; try a single one this time. Nothing like a solid new love affair to forget an old one."

"But it can't be over," I argued. "Things just can't end like that."

"How'd they end with Al?"

"That was different."

"How?"

"Al didn't mean as much to me."

"Bullshit."

It astounded me to remember I had cared as intensely for Al as I now did for Scott. And I had solemnly vowed to grab the next man by the balls and run things my way. What had gone wrong?

Since Nicole had taken the week off to be with her daughter, the work load was overwhelming. I dug in, but with little heart. Freddy wasn't much help. "It's my patron," he complained. "Says he's in love with me, wants to be around all the time. He's even thinking, God forbid, of leaving his wife."

"You have all the luck," I sighed.

"Garrison is rather being a shithead, isn't he?" noted Freddy. "Why don't you just march in there and tell him to—" Freddy paused to think of something to tell him.

"Okay. Tell him what?" The door to Scott's office opened. He walked through the office, a cold look in his eyes, out the door without noticing either of us.

"Tell him to shove it up his ass," suggested Freddy.

"That's what started it," I sighed.

"What's with the big prick?" asked Helen, who passed Scott coming through the doorway. "Not gettin' enough?" She winked at me. She saw the expression on my face. "Aw, honey, he's not worth it. Listen, I've got this terrific Greek."

"No thanks, Helen."

"Not that greasy kid. This one's rich and good-looking. Hung like he's had a silicone injection. Priscilla's been eyein' him for weeks, but he likes a girl with some smarts. Priscilla's so dumb she'd fuck up a two-car funeral."

"Hey, anybody hear from Nicole?" asked Freddy. We shook our heads.

"I'm worried about her," said Helen. "The whole thing ain't right. I've got a terrible feeling in here." She hit a spot under one of her massive boobs.

That night Nicole called me at home. It was the first time I'd ever heard from her outside work. "You busy right now?" she asked. There was a tone of urgency in her voice. "Can I stop by," she hesitated, "and bring my daughter?"

It was an odd request, coming from Nicole. Although we had been friends as coworkers, there remained a distance. She kept apart from all of us.

I almost didn't recognize her at the door. The look of soft femininity she carefully cultivated had vanished. Her red hair was pulled back tightly, and there was no makeup to cover the circles under her obviously tired eyes.

The daughter, Jeanne, still wore the look of sleepy indolence I had noticed that morning in the office. She quietly took a chair, lit up a casual cigarette and watched the smoke she was exhaling.

Nicole began some nervous conversation. "I like your apartment. It's small, but it does have character. Don't you like it, Jeanne? Look at the view.

Emily, it's simply spectacular." Jeanne rose to get a better look, and stood at the window.

"Atmosphere is so important where you live and work," continued Nicole. "That's one thing Ralph Gordon will never understand." She watched her daughter, who sat seemingly mesmerized with the lights of the city. "If only he'd throw some money into furnishing that office." Her voice trailed off.

"We might as well be selling insurance instead of exotic vacations." I tried to pull Nicole back. "It wouldn't take much money. Some rattan chairs, a few pictures to give it a tropical look."

Nicole's face brightened, "Yes, but Ralph doesn't understand the psychological side of this business. His theory is, if you make it cheap enough, people will buy."

"He hasn't done too badly on that," I suggested. I thought it odd not to include her daughter in the conversation some way, but Nicole seemed to be relieved talking business.

"Emily, he could double, no, triple his sales with a little packaging. Look at our tour brochures. That's why we get so little response from our mailers. Once someone comes into the office, they're hooked, only because you and I are good saleswomen. Otherwise they'd be out the door, paying more money for the same thing."

"It would be easier if we had something to show the customers. All we have to sell is a fluff of imagination. Even our vouchers look like bank statements. Could it cost that much more to have them printed up on brightly colored paper?"

Nicole shook her head. "It doesn't cost that much more to have our brochures printed up nicely. The airlines provide free shells with full-color photographs. All Ralph has to pay is the printing costs."

We might have been speaking Croatian for all the recognition Jeanne gave us. She seemed not to hear at all.

"Have you ever suggested any of this to Ralph?" I asked.

Nicole laughed. "Ralph Gordon has his own way of doing business. Some day when I own my own —you know, you and I really think alike when it comes to running a travel agency. I'm continually amazed at what a good grasp you have of this business. You're really not much older than my daughter."

We both looked at Jeanne staring off into the night. "Honey," Nicole called to her. "Come on in and talk to us for a while." Jeanne strolled slowly back in and sat down.

"How do you like Los Angeles?" I asked her politely.

"Fine."

"Have you seen much of the sights?"

"No."

"We haven't had much time," apologized Nicole, "and her boyfriend is in town."

"He's taking me to Disneyland tomorrow," Jeanne said without expression. "Wow, I really hear that's a trip when you're—" She paused and looked at her mother.

"Stoned?" I supplied.

Jeanne suddenly looked on me as an ally. "You got any grass?" she asked hopefully. "I've been trying to explain to my mother. I mean, she's really cool about a lot of things, but she's never turned on. I'd love to turn her on." Nicole looked at me in desperation. I realized why she had brought her daughter over. I'd told her about the morning I'd discovered Al sprawled out on the living room floor. "For God's sake, Jeanne!" I turned on her. "I don't have any shit around here. What the hell are you fooling around with that for?"

Jeanne wasn't prepared for my outburst. It was cutting into her high. She lifted up her chin and looked at me defiantly. Perhaps it was the wrong approach. I wasn't a psychologist, but she would have the benefit of my honesty. "Did my mother tell you to say that?"

"Of course not. I had no idea except that you sauntered into my apartment with the glazed look in your eyes that I've seen often enough in my life. My boyfriend used to greet me that way night after night. Then one morning I went to see him and there was—no look in his eyes."

I let the silence ride a few moments.

"He OD'd?" she asked quietly.

"You ever seen that?" I asked her.

She shook her head.

"You will. Pretty sight. But maybe you won't see it. Depends on what kind of shit you're into. It could be you." I was deliberately harsh to cut through her fog.

"Did he die?" she asked, her eyes very wide.

I looked away and walked to the window. I

knew the impact I was making depended upon her believing my boyfriend had died. I refused to answer.

"My father died," Jeanne said softly in a high, thin, childish voice. It made me wonder if it weren't only the drugs that made her so strange. "But I'm pregnant. I got pregnant the week after he died and my boyfriend tells me that my child will be my father reincarnated. Even if it's a girl."

"Jeanne—" Nicole bit her lower lip in desperation.

26

Nicole met me for lunch the next day. "*I tried to* talk Jeanne out of going to Disneyland with that creep. Oh, God, Emily, you've never seen such a mess of a kid—dirty fingernails, long, greasy hair. And he's a pipsqueak of a guy. How can she stand to get in bed with him? I've never had a man under six feet."

"What's so magic about the number six?" I asked.

"My stepmother told me, and she's right. Men under six feet have terrible complexes. It's best to avoid them. I think if I could pry her loose from this hippie freak, I could talk some sense into her. At least it would cut down on her supply of whatever she's taking."

"Why don't you forbid her to see him?"

"That," she said, "is what the bitch in New Orleans tried to do. I finally broke down and called her last night. God, how I hated that woman. How much energy I expended in despising the woman who stole my husband away!" She laughed, "Husbands are never stolen, Emily, they're given away. But now she's got it all back. The poor pediatrician, destined to care for other people's children, never could have any of her own. Jeanne's all she's got left in the world, the only thing she cares about.

Oh, shit, I'm feeling sorry for her! But they had no right, no right at all to tell my child I was dead. That's one of the reasons she is so fucked up now. If her mother isn't really dead, then maybe her father isn't. They were very close. And then this kid came along and filled her head with drugs and nonsense."

"How's your husband handling all this?"

She sighed. "We've had our differences, but he's really coming through for me. What a rock. He may just be the one to reach her. He's trying hard to be her father. He's a good man, a damn good man. I don't deserve it."

"Of course you deserve it!" I defended her. I was feeling the awesome weight of responsibility for bringing up her spirits.

She shook her head. "I'm a rotten wife. But it's partly his fault. He knew me going in. Thought I'd change. I made him promise to let me keep my freedom, go out when I choose, have lovers when I wanted."

"He *knows* about your lovers?"

"I told him if he didn't like it, he could leave. He knows they don't mean anything—they're just a way of maintaining my independence."

"Do you love him, Nicole?"

She nodded. "As much as I can ever love any man." Then she said sadly, "Emily, I grew a shell around myself at an early age, a coat of armor for protection. A man can make dents in that, but he can't pierce it. I'm trying hard now, especially since Jeanne is here. He'd like to see us become a—

family." She gave a futile little gesture as if to wave away the thought.

"Well, you're about to be a grandmother," I joked.

"No, maybe not," she said, suddenly happier. "My husband had a long talk with her when we got home last night. She's agreed, at least, to consider an abortion."

"I wish I had a good abortionist to recommend, but the only thing I'd recommend to mine is castration with a dull blade."

"There's a gynecologist in the Valley. We have an appointment to see him tomorrow. For all I know, she only thinks she's pregnant. This kid has her thinking black is white and day is night. How's work?" She was obviously tired of talking about her troubles.

"It's impossible in there without you. By the way," I added, because I knew it would please her, "I've been reading the *Wall Street Journal* religiously."

"And what have you learned?"

"Give me fifty thousand dollars and I can make a killing for you in a cattle-feeding program. Then we'll stick it all in tax-free municipal bonds."

"Keep reading," she laughed, "and pick on some programs your own size."

I thought about Nicole that afternoon at work. I wondered what life would bring me, if I'd ever develop a suit of armor to protect me from the piercing swords of the Als and Scotts in this world.

27

"*Have you hardened yourself to life's slings and* arrows, Freddy?" I asked as we sat in front of his fire, sipping cognac that night.

"You just can't lose your sense of humor about things," he advised.

"Do you think God has a sense of humor?"

"Yeah, a sadistic one. God is a pervert. Mark my words. He probably runs around exposing himself to all the saints. When I get to heaven, I'm going to go down as the first one to ever give God a blowjob."

"You're an ambitious fucker, Freddy. Just think, it might change the whole course of history. Maybe that's what's been wrong with the world all along. How could someone dump a black plague on humanity after a good blow job?"

"Beats me," agreed Freddy. "How are your blow-jobs progressing? Did my instructions help?"

"Oh yes, and I've picked up a lot of new things along the way."

"Like what?" Freddy was intrigued.

"I'd have to show you," I smiled and rolled over on my back.

"I can't imagine there's something I haven't tried at least once," he flirted, kissing me lightly on the lips. I smiled up at him and ran a hand down his chest. I stopped at his cock. It was already hard. Firelight reflected in his eyes. He unbuttoned my blouse and let his tongue wander over my breasts. "I'd forgotten how nice a woman's breasts can feel," he murmured.

"Wait'll you feel my gorgeous pussy," I teased.

"A gorgeously tight pussy," he said as we began to make love.

"Not too tight for you, darling?"

"That's like being too rich," he laughed. We were enjoying this time together. It was as though we were at an amusement park. We laughed and giggled, teased and played. Freddy was sensual as a kitten, but basically passive. I was having fun, but I never forgot where or who I was. Scott had whirled me in a cloud of passion up to other galaxies. I would never be the same.

Freddy opened a bottle of Mumms champagne afterward, to celebrate. "You know what I like best about your tits?" he asked, raising a glass. "They're perfect size. Just enough to fill a champagne glass."

"And your cock is just big enough to cork the bottle!"

"We make a cute couple," he laughed. "Too bad I don't like women."

"You gave a splendid imitation of it."

"But, darling." He hugged me. "You're an exception. You're so butch. Next thing I hear, you'll probably be a flaming bulldyke."

"You say the sweetest things. Seriously, though, what did you think about the blowjob? Now, don't spare me. I can take it."

He took a thoughtful sip of champagne and raised his eyebrows. "Not bad. No, not bad at all. For a woman."

"You fucker, you never had it so good."

"Don't count on it," he laughed.

"Your patron, what's he like in bed?"

He pulled me down on the floor and put our champagne glasses aside. "Not nearly as good as you, darling."

Strange how a few months before I had wanted two men, thinking them both inaccessible. Now I had had them both. It was, all considered, a hollow conquest.

Scott was the only one I thought about, even while making love to Freddy. Each night I went to bed, hoping to be awakened by a phone call. When he passed by me without a word or a glance, my chest caved in. I thought I could never suffer as much after Al, but Scott cut even deeper. How could hurt build you a suit of armor? I barely had a layer of skin to cover my frayed nerves.

When the doorbell to my apartment rang the next night, I hoped, half-scared, it might be Scott —drunk and wanting me as he had that other night he told me he was married. To my dismay it was my cousin, Cindy.

"Got anything to drink in this dump?" she stumbled in. All the years I'd known her, Cindy never had a hair out of place, not even when she got up in the morning. Tonight she was not only disheveled, but without makeup. I poured her the last of my scotch and she spooned the ice out into the sink. "I need this shit full strength. Scotch without the rocks; a marriage on them. Poof! Just like that. Emily, I haven't been such a bad wife, have I?"

"You and Bob?" My mouth fell open.

"You didn't answer my question. Have I been such a bad wife?"

I shrugged my shoulders.

"Goddamn it, Emily, this is no time for honesty. Tell me I wasn't such a bad wife."

"You were a wonderful wife, Cindy."

"No, I wasn't. I must not have been or he wouldn't be leaving me." She sniffed. Her eyes were red from crying. "I wanted him home every night for dinner. I've always dreamed of having a man home every night for dinner. When I was a kid, the table always seemed so empty. Just Mother and me. And she was so lonely."

It was disturbing to see Cindy this way. She was always so sure of herself, in control. Her life had been planned carefully to the last detail, now it was crumbling at the foundations. What could be knocking it over?

"Another woman."

"Did he tell you?"

"No. He just said he didn't love me anymore. That's standard. They always say that when there's another woman. And he hasn't slept with me since Christmas. Oh Emily, I did such silly things to entice him, things like you read in the magazines—perfumes, negligees, candlelit dinners. Do you have any more scotch?" She gulped down the last drop and frowned into the bottom of the glass.

The cupboard was bare. At my salary, liquor was low priority on a shopping list. I suggested we walk over to Freddy's. He always had a good supply of booze and easy conversation. There was nothing Cindy could do in her state but feel sorry for herself and evoke my sympathy. Between my own sorry state and Nicole's, I was all evoked out.

"Freddy's?" She moaned. "You know I can't stand fags."

"He's bi, if that makes you feel any better."

"Bullshit, he is."

"Cindy, I had him the other night."

She looked at me in amazement. "I've got to hand it to you, little cousin," she said with admiration. "All right. I'll go over there. If he fucked you, he can't be all bad. And I do need a drink."

Since it was a Friday night, I didn't bother calling first. The patron was never there on weekends. Freddy was glad to see me, but I could tell he didn't care much for Cindy. Nonetheless, he made an effort. Freddy always made an effort. He was a social creature who shone as a host. He might despise someone, but that person would never feel it as a guest in his home. It was his holy sanctuary, where rudeness amounted to blasphemy.

After a few drinks, he was able to loosen up Cindy to where they were even laughing and talking about his plants. "Your fern is getting too much light," she told him. "Move it over here. And you've got to spray your ivy. It's getting infested with those little red spider mites."

I congratulated myself for bringing her up there.

Freddy was a good distraction for her troubles. I left them chatting happily in the living room and went upstairs to use Freddy's bathroom.

There was a yellow Kodak photo envelope on his dresser, with some color prints protruding out. I'm not the snoopy type, but curiosity got the best of me.

There was a good shot of Freddy in swim trunks by the pool, another of Freddy diving. There was a middle-aged, balding man in a lounge chair, also in swim trunks. *This must be Freddy's patron,* I thought. I looked for a closer shot of him, fascinated to finally catch a glimpse of the wealthy man who—my heart stopped. Suddenly it all fit together: why Freddy had never mentioned his lover by name; Freddy's dislike for Cindy; Cindy's fight with Bob—

I heard a car pull up outside. The door slammed. Footsteps down the wooden walkway to Freddy's house. My God, I had to get Cindy out of there! I rushed downstairs. A key was turning in the front door. I held my breath. Maybe it wasn't. Maybe someone was just dropping in.

"Oh, good fuck," whispered Freddy. Cindy turned and screamed.

"So my wife and my lover have finally met." Bob was smashed even more to the gills than his wife. He weaved his way over to where Cindy and Freddy stood together like statues, sliding an arm around them both. "Now this is a joke, isn't it?" he laughed nervously.

Cindy crawled out from under his arm as though

he were diseased. "You fucking cocksucker," she muttered under her breath.

"You see?" Bob turned to Freddy. "Suck one lousy cock and you're labeled for life." Freddy had the sense to keep his mouth shut.

It was incongruous, seeing Bob there with his arm around Freddy. It was obscene and awesome. I imagined them naked and embracing, as Freddy and I had been. An entire love scene passed before my eyes. Bob was leaving Cindy. He was in love with Freddy. Freddy had made love to me the night before. I looked at Cindy. Evidently her mind had been following the same sequence.

"Don't stand there so smug, Bob," she said between her teeth. "When you're home with me, he's here fucking Emily." Without waiting to see the devastation written on her husband's face, she bolted out the door. I was right behind her.

She ran wildly up the street through the Hollywood Hills. I kept just far enough behind to keep an eye on her. I knew the physical effort of running would sober her up, get some of the grief out of her system. I glanced up at the stars now and then, wondering what possible configuration caused this mess. Maybe Freddy was right. God *was* a pervert.

At the top of the hill, Cindy stopped out of breath and threw up her scotch. "That feels better," she admitted. We sat down on a curb and looked out over the city. Millions of lights shimmering above and below us. I thought of that night a hundred years ago when I lost my virginity to Al

in the Berkeley Hills, with the lights of San Francisco twinkling in the distance.

"It's like the whole city's having an orgasm,"
I said philosophically.

"Oh, please." Cindy began to laugh. "Let's not
talk about sex!" The absurdity of it all struck us,
and we laughed and cried until our bellies ached.

28

Monday morning caught everyone at the office looking like a hangover. Even Helen was in a dark mood. "They're letting my old man out next week on good behavior," she moaned.

"I should think that would cheer you up," said Nicole.

"I'm supposed to go to Greece next week. Now I gotta sit home and get the house cleaned up. I tell you, I love the guy, but husbands can be a pain in the ass."

"Tell me about it," said Freddy. He turned to me sheepishly. "How's Cindy doing?"

"Not bad," I said, "considering. She spent all Saturday buying out Saks Fifth Avenue before he closes the account. This morning she made an appointment with the best divorce attorney in Beverly Hills."

"She'll get a good settlement," said Freddy. "It's that insurance I told you about—having a kid. He's crazy about the little monster. Probably bring him over weekends after he moves in."

"He's moving in with you?" asked Helen. "What happened to the precious freedom you're always bragging about?"

Freddy shrugged his shoulders and smiled sadly.

"You have to give up some things, darling, when you get married."

Helen and Nicole both sighed simultaneously. Marriage was like a club they all belonged to. Like the sorority. We used to complain about it, but nobody ever resigned.

"What's happening with your daughter?" I asked Nicole.

"Ah," she said brightly, "Jeanne told that Frankenstein monster to take a hike. I've got my husband to thank for that. It's amazing what a nice kid she is off all the stuff that boy was supplying. She's even thinking of going back to New Orleans to finish high school." There was a note of weariness in Nicole's voice. I suspected she almost wished her daughter would go back. Nicole had been too long without the burden of parental responsibility to have it so dramatically thrust upon her.

The office had gone through a subtle change in the last week. No longer was there any privacy. We were all caught up in our own personal tragedies, yet drawn together in mutual concern as closely as the last survivors of a shipwreck. Only Priscilla and Mr. Gordon remained aloof from our disasters.

Priscilla hadn't spoken to me since I took Jim Johnson away from her at the Christmas party. I think she secretly delighted in seeing me stomped upon by Scott Garrison.

Mr. Gordon would never involve himself in the internal intrigues of his office, unless an employee's work was affected. It was a marvel that Royal Beverly rolled on so smoothly when all the cogs in the wheel were coming unglued. Maybe the travel business was, as Scott suggested, the ultimate escape—as if through the mere act of telling people about a tropical paradise, we could write our own ticket there. Selling travel was a blessed refuge, an eternal constant in an erratic world. It thrilled me to think that I might have stumbled by chance onto a secret of life that had mystified mankind for centuries. One can face any problem, no matter how severe, if one has the option of escaping it altogether.

Scott was spending less and less time at work. That day he didn't show up until almost closing time. Everyone but Nicole and I had left. He passed by my desk as usual, without a word and went into his office. I caught Nicole watching me. She knew what I was feeling. A few moments later she went into Scott's office and closed the door. It was more than I could stand. I grabbed my coat and escaped out the door.

The phone was ringing when I got home. It was Scott. "I'm at the Polo Lounge. Come on down."

"Okay," was all I could answer before he hung up. My heart was pounding. *This must be it,* I thought excitedly, *the reconciliation.* I tried to think like Cindy. She would be cold and aloof at first, let him sweat it out, then take him back reluctantly, on her terms.

Seeing him sitting in the Polo Lounge, I lost my resolve. I was aloof as a springer spaniel puppy. He sat in a corner booth, staring at his drink, the familiar look of quiet brooding on his face. He glanced at me when I sat down without smiling.

"What're you drinking?" he asked, then looked away to find the waiter. This wouldn't be an easy reconciliation.

We sat in his self-inflicted silence until my drink arrived and I decided to bring him back to the world of the living. Office gossip was a safe topic, and at the moment, plentiful enough to carry us through an entire evening.

"What do you think about Helen's husband getting out of jail?" I began lightly.

"I hadn't thought about it at all," he said, staring blankly across the room.

"Sure going to put a curb on her social life," I joked. "For a married woman, she really gets around."

"Sure does," he commented, and pulled his silence up again like a cloak over his shoulders.

"Hear what happened to Cindy over the weekend?" I tried again.

"No."

"Well, she found her husband was keeping Freddy, of all people."

More silence.

"Don't you think it's horrendous?"

No comment.

"What if you were in her place? What if you found out your wife was a dyke?" He glared at me.

"My first wife was a dyke. The violinist she ran off with was a woman." I was regretting my try at a comeback. Why did he invite me here this evening? Just to make me miserable? I looked around at a room filled with gentle banter, smiles, and secret intrigues. I would give office gossip one more try. What else did we have to say to each other?

"Nicole's evidently having a rough time with her daughter."

"Oh, really?" This subject seemed to spark some interest.

"I guess it's hard having a kid around after so many years," I continued. "Do you think her daughter will end up staying here?"

Scott pondered the question. "I doubt it," he said finally. "Children, even husbands, require a lot of attention. Nicole is a hell of a woman, but she'll never see beyond herself." There was a tone in his voice that made me think of his mother's rose garden. I felt the sharp pang of jealousy.

"I think you've always been a little in love with Nicole," I teased.

"Emily." He looked directly into my eyes for the first time that night. "I'm not only in love with Nicole, I'm married to her."

29

It seems impossible now, looking back, that I wouldn't have guessed it, but the realization of that moment fell on me like an avalanche of granite. Everything Nicole had ever said about her husband came back to me. I rushed out of the Polo Lounge before Scott could see my tears. Tony, who was standing at the door, came after me. He caught me as I was about to give my check to the car attendant. "No," he said, slipping the card back into my purse. "Taxi, please," he ordered the attendant. "You're too upset to drive," he said gently. "Do you need any money for the cab?" I shook my head and gave the cab driver Cindy's address. I didn't even want to chance Scott following me home.

"So you were just a ploy to make Nicole jealous," Cindy surmised when I broke the news. "I must admit it was pretty clever, you working right there under her nose. I bet that put a damper on her act."

"Nicole!" I said angrily. "She was coming on like my best friend." It would take hours for my tears to dry up that night.

"You can't trust anyone," sighed Cindy. "I'll bet she was jealous as hell."

"Nicole? Of me?"

"If he'd picked someone like Priscilla, Nicole would never have considered it a threat. But you, you're bright and beautiful, and you've got the one thing Nicole doesn't have anymore—youth. And a certain appealing innocence. It must have driven her up a wall. She's the type who can dish it out, but she can't take it."

"No, she was too busy with that banker to care. She can't respect Scott. He's got all this money, but he doesn't know how to earn it on his own."

"She doesn't respect him," corrected Cindy, "because she dumps all over him and he puts up with it. He revels in punishment. The only way you could have kept him was to make him suffer. Look at his first wife, a dyke, yet. Then he hooks up with a woman who flaunts her affairs in front of him. It probably all stems back to his mother. I bet she neglected him when he was young."

"Then she died."

"Deserted him!" Cindy snapped her fingers. "That's it. He needs a woman to desert him like his mother did. That's what you should have done, Emily. You didn't play the pattern through."

"You're full of shit," I decided. "One session with a shrink and you're analyzing everyone."

"I also majored in psychology. You didn't make that man suffer sufficiently. I'm finally beginning to understand that about men. Like Bob. His mother always used to play on his sense of guilt. She'd weep and carry on if he didn't call twice a week."

"You're trying to tell me Bob *likes* feeling guilty?"

"Of course not. He's just used to it. He wanted me to make him feel guilty. He was pushing me in that direction. I used to harass him about staying home more often, then I stopped. Too much effort. That's where your friend, Freddy, had the advantage. What could make a man feel more guilty than a clandestine affair with another man? Wow, he could feel guilty to me, to little Bobby, to his mother, *and* to his executive image. A whole shitload of tailor-made guilt. No way I could compete with Freddy.

"It was like in college when that Sigma Chi left me for a mousy little librarian who had only one leg. She was dying of bone cancer. This guy got off on sympathy. How could I, the sweetheart of Sigma Chi, make him feel sorry enough for me to compete with that?"

"You could have cut off your leg," I suggested.

She ignored my comment and continued. "It's the same thing with Nicole's daughter. He left you the minute her daughter showed up, right?"

"I was in competition with that fucked-up little drug addict?"

"Symbolically. The little addict gave Scott a chance to prove himself useful. At last Nicole really needed him for something. She certainly had no use for a husband. Motherhood may be a strong instinct, but it requires some talent. Nicole Randall could probably sell capitalism to Castro—have him on his knees begging for it—but she has no idea how to parent. Scott finally found the perfect way to get to her. He could be a mother to her child.

Having an affair with you wasn't nearly so effective. He's got her by the balls now."

I sighed and mixed another drink for me and Cindy. Her psychological lectures were always bewildering. "You remember that night in the sorority I was fixing you wine coolers for my initiation points? Life was so uncomplicated then." We burst simultaneously into song:

> As sisters all we fuck
> Whenever we're in luck. . . .

Our voices trailed off into the nostalgic haze and we fell silent. "I don't think I'll ever be young and appealingly innocent again," I said sadly.

"That," said Cindy wryly, "was just a figure of speech. Neither one of us was ever innocent. Young and inexperienced, maybe. We're all destined to repeat our mistakes, the mistakes of our elders. Pete and Repeat were brothers, Pete died. Which one was left? Repeat. Pete and Repeat were brothers—

"Look at me, I planned it all out and I'm in the same situation my mother was in. You're playing out the same game plan with Scott as you did with Al. You should have bowed out the minute that guy told you he was into history."

"No. I won't accept that. There's got to be a way out. Otherwise the whole universe is just a giant pinball machine and we're all tiny silver balls banged and tossed around by neon levers, eventually dropping back into the same old slot from whence we came, only to be shot out again and again by whichever mad, perverted fucker happens to be in control.

"What'd your shrink advise you to do?"

"Rebuild my self-image, for starters," said Cindy emphatically.

"I thought you already did that at Saks."

"It helped, of course, but the problem is more complex. I was not only rejected for myself, but as a woman. It's as though there were something lacking in me."

"It's called a penis."

"Yes. Now I must redefine myself."

"How?"

She thought a moment. "I think I'll have a fat juicy affair for starters. I'd love to have one with Freddy. Wouldn't that just set Bob off?"

"Sounds more like revenge than redefinition. Besides, Freddy is rather complacent in bed. Fat and juicy isn't his style."

"You're right. And fags have never appealed to me. I think I'll stick to my attorney. He's ripe— just turned forty, that dangerous age. Starting to lose some hair, afraid he'll go impotent and ugly, and all he'll have left is his wife. He's taking me to dinner tomorrow night. You'd absolutely love him, Emily—the most gorgeous thing I've ever seen in a pair of wing-tipped shoes. I've always maintained you can tell a lot about a man by his shoes."

While Cindy basked in her new-found freedom and redefinitions, Freddy adjusted badly to his new shackles. "At least he's out of town a lot," he confided to me at work the next morning. I was surprised to learn the business trips were real, not man-

ufactured excuses to see Freddy during the week.
"I'm sure he hits every gay bar between here and
New York, but he expects me to sit home every
night and wait for him. I had a hell of a time convincing him that you and I never had an affair. By
the way, what are you doing tonight? He'll be out of
town until Thursday."

I was about to reply when Nicole walked in.
Freddy glared at her. "Cunt," he said to her. "You
might have told us all at the outset."

"It's none of your business, Freddy," she said
coolly. "Emily, can I take you to lunch today?"
Her voice rang with remorse.

"Why not?" I said, trying to feign indifference.
I was less interested in her apologies than in hear-
ing her side of the story. Curiosity is a powerful
motivating force and I desperately wanted to hear
something that would prove Cindy's pseudo-
psychology wrong.

"I wanted to tell you," said Nicole at lunch.

"But there was a cork in your throat," I said
coldly.

"It wasn't my place, damnit! You'd think I was
coming on like the jealous wife. I still think of
you as a friend, Emily. I could see he was hurting
you. I finally convinced him last night to tell you.
He wanted to let it drop and die out; he figured you'd
lose interest if he was cool enough."

"How touching. You only had my well-being at
heart. This is bullshit, Nicole. Let's face it. You
could care less about my feelings. And Scott was
just using me all along to make you jealous."

Nicole's eyes widened. "You did make me jealous," she said quietly. "None of the others did. He had to pick someone I liked and respected. We were going to split. Especially after this last hypocritical year when he came to work for Ralph. I always felt he had arranged it just so he could keep an eye on me."

"And you gave him plenty to look at." I thought of the bank manager.

"But then he started with you," she continued, "and I realized I didn't want to lose him after all. Then Jeanne arrived. He'll stay with me as long as she's here."

I studied the determined expression on her face.

"You see, Emily, I need him."

I could cut off a leg or adopt a heart-rending Ethiopian orphan, but I could never compete with that tangle of interdependence. Nicole needed Jeanne to keep Scott, who needed Jeanne to keep Nicole; and Jeanne needed them both to get back at her stepmother in New Orleans. More than anything, it irked me that Cindy had been right.

"But," added Nicole with a bright smile, "if you can manage to put your personal feelings aside, I've got an exciting proposition to make you. I wanted to tell you about it before, then all this happened. I'm opening my own agency and I want you to come to work for me."

"You're out of your fucking mind."

"Don't be so hasty. I'll double your salary. You look shocked. You shouldn't be. It would take two employees to take your place. You're worth every penny."

My conscience told me to turn her down right away. Greed was trying its best to make a prostitute out of me. "I'll think it over," I said, and smiled. Was I already warming to the idea?

30

Lucky Cindy. She only had to rebuild a self-image and redefine herself. I had to make a practical decision that would affect my entire future. I sat down that night to make a list of the advantages and disadvantages of Nicole's offer.

On the disadvantage side I listed:

1. Can't trust Nicole. She's ruthless.
2. Scott will be involved.
3. I'd have to work twice as hard for twice the pay, knowing Nicole.
4. Her business could fail and leave me unemployed.

The advantages I saw were:

1. Nicole might be honest with me now that everything was out.
2. It's all over with Scott, anyway.
3. I'd have twice as much money.
4. Nicole would never let a business fail.
5. I wouldn't let it fail.
6. I'd have twice as much money. (Greed was figuring heavily in my decision, so I listed it twice.)
7. I would never have to deal with Al again.

I called Freddy and asked if I could come over. He knew this business. I needed another opinion.

"Uh, darling, Bob is here. Didn't go out of town after all," said Freddy.

"Good, then I can get his opinion, too," I said. My hanky-panky days with Freddy were over. I'd lost all stomach for extramarital intrigues.

Bob had made himself at home. He sauntered around in swim trunks, paunch hanging out, as he did at Cindy's. There was something sickeningly familiar in his behavior, but I don't know why I'd expected a huge change in him. He was no more obtrusive an entity here than one of Freddy's houseplants. Freddy was the surprise.

He flitted and darted to and fro, pursing his lips, making Bob help him with the ice trays, open a can of olives. His voice seemed to have raised half an octave, whining more than usual. "Oh!" He gave an exasperated little sigh. "This house is so dirty. Bob doesn't rinse off a single plate. He splatters shaving cream all over the sink in the bathroom."

"Why don't you get a maid?" I suggested.

"A maid! I *am* the maid," he laughed. He mopped up the water spilled from the ice trays. "A woman's work is never done."

Bob smiled at him, indulgently amused. It was a loving look I'd never see him give Cindy. "Emily?" He took me aside. "I'm glad you came over here tonight. I was always fond of you—the only one of her relatives I liked. I hope you'll remain one of our friends."

"Sure, Bob, thanks." I watched Freddy scurry around the living room, shoving coasters under our drinks.

"So Nicole's finally going to open her own

agency. About time," Bob continued. "Hell of a businesswoman, from what you and Freddy have said. Who's putting up the money?"

"She is, I guess, and probably her husband."

"Nicole has friends in the banking business," added Freddy.

"The travel industry has always interested me," said Bob. "I've often thought it would be kind of nice to own an agency. How about me setting up you and Freddy in business?"

"No, Bob," Freddy interrupted. "You just keep working at your job. I have no desire to run a business. In fact, I just may retire altogether now that you're living here. Being a housewife is a full-time job. At least with the mess you make."

Freddy sent Bob to the liquor store to buy some more Courvoisier. "Get one of those *big* bottles this time," said Freddy. "You know, family-size."

Once Bob was out the door, Freddy calmed down his act. "Love is hell." He sank down on the couch beside me. "How's that gorgeous tight little pussy of yours holding up?" He shoved a hand down my pants.

"It's going into cold storage. Maybe I'll will it to science. How can you cheat on your honeymoon?"

Freddy raised his eyebrows. "Don't knock it. Money makes up for a lot of things. You'll end up working for Nicole. And it won't be for the kind affection she's inspired in you."

31

It would be hard to tell Ralph I was leaving. I dreaded that more than anything. In spite of his aloofness, I felt a certain unspoken kinship with this man. Our relationship was simple. I had produced money for him and he had rewarded me with it. I felt sorry for him. He was losing his two best money-producers.

He looked very small behind his desk, small and defenseless. How could I do this to him?

"How much did she offer you?" He didn't wait for me to begin.

"Double what I get here."

He sat back and looked at me for a long moment, trying to decide, I supposed, if I was worth every penny.

"It's purely economic, Ralph," I apologized. "I really prefer working for you, but—"

"There are going to be a lot of changes around here," he interrupted. "You know Scott Garrison is leaving, too." I nodded. "I'm going to need a general manager, not like Garrison was, but someone who can operate this business, like Nicole. You've got a good mind, Emily, an uncanny good sense about making money. Some of these girls come in here thinking it's a glamour business; they believe all that crap we put in tour brochures. But you understand it's a business, like anything else. Your age doesn't bother me. Hell, I owned my own company at your age. I don't want to lose you. How would you like to be general manager of Royal Beverly?"

"At how much?" I'd heard about bosses who doled out titles in place of hard cash.

"I'll give you what Nicole offered."

"She also mentioned a percentage of the commissions." I lied, but I think Ralph knew it. Still, he admired that kind of balls.

"I'll give you a third of the net on whatever you bring in yourself."

"How much control will I have? I have a lot of ideas that—" of course included getting rid of that dead weight, Priscilla.

"Make me a list, we'll discuss them tomorrow." I shook hands with him and smiled. "By the way," he added, "Scott's leaving his office the way it is, decor and all. If you want it like that, it's up to you."

"We need a storage room." I motioned to the tour brochures on his floor. "And a photo-copier. Our files are bulging. Your general manager should be out front where she can see what's going on. We should get rid of the reception room entirely and add another salesperson."

He cracked a smile. "I won't be able to keep you long. You'll want your own business, too, one of these days."

"Not if you make me a partner."

The benevolent smile left his face. I'd try that another time.

I left his office, my chest puffed out, visions of sugarplums dancing in my head. "Nicole," I approached her desk. "I've come to a decision. I'm going to stay here."

"It's because of Scott, isn't it?" she asked.

Before I could answer, Jeanne walked through the door. She looked very much like her mother at that moment. There was self-assurance on her face, and a calm composure. The bright eagerness of youth was in her eyes.

"Mom," she said, "I'd like to talk to you and Scott for a moment." They disappeared into Scott's office.

I watched the clock. The moment stretched into half an hour. When they emerged, Scott and Jeanne were smiling. Nicole was pale. While she busied herself with some things on the desk, Scott's eyes met mine for a brief moment. I looked away. Those eyes brought back too many painful memories. Even my new business conquests couldn't erase that. The three of them—the little family—walked out the door.

I glanced over to Nicole's desk. There were ticket coupons. I looked closer. A one-way ticket. So Jeanne was going back to New Orleans.

32

No, mustn't think about it, I told myself. Didn't Scott say he loved Nicole. It was probably her imagination, thinking Scott would only stay because of Jeanne. And even if he did leave her, why would he come back to me? He only needed me to make her jealous. I had outworn my usefulness.

Yet he had called me that night and wanted to come over. I sat on my patio, taking deep breaths, making lists of changes for Ralph.

Try to act casual, natural. The doorbell. Scott's wonderful body in the doorway. *Smile. He is nervous, too.* My hands shake fixing a drink. My face reddens. *Why is he here? I'm so afraid to hope.*

"Nicole thinks it's because of me, that you won't work for her," he began. So that was it. He was an emissary of good will. Had she sent him to seduce me into it?

"She's wrong," I said coldly.

"If it is the reason," he said, ignoring me, "and I know you've got too much pride to admit it, I'm not going to be working with her. I'm getting out of this business."

"What are you going to do?"

"Go back to school. Work on a doctorate."

"History?"

"What else?" He smiled.

"Well, I hate to disappoint you and Nicole, but my reasons are purely economic. Ralph offered me more money and the position of general manager. You are no longer a factor in my life."

He looked at me with wicked cat eyes and smiled.

"Fuck off, Garrison. I mean it."

He ran his hand down my arm. It made me shudder.

"No longer a factor?"

I pointed to my head, "Up here, at least." I jumped up from the couch and walked across the room. Better to keep my distance.

"Where are you going to school?" I tried to change the subject.

"Greece, maybe, to do research. I want to get into Greek history."

"You should have been fooling around with Helen, then." I stopped for a moment as the idea hit me. "Then you are leaving Nicole?"

He nodded. "I stuck around to help while she needed me."

"Needed you to put up the money for her travel agency," I added sarcastically.

"Don't be too hard on Nicole. She thinks very highly of you. It wasn't her fault you got involved with me."

"But if she hadn't been screwing you around, you'd never have looked at me."

He was silent, thoughtful for a moment. "At first, maybe, but not later. You can't really believe I'd spend all that time with you just to make her jealous?"

I was fighting back tears. "Oh shit, I don't know anymore. I only wish you'd get out of my life. Go to Greece or Timbuktu or the shores of Tripoli or—"

"I might go to USC or UCLA."

"How nice. And plan package history tours for Nicole's travel agency? The history professor's guided tours. I'll be sure to recommend your cruises. Why, ancient history will literally come alive for your students." I looked at Scott through my tirade. There was the little boy, his mother playing Chopin while he wandered alone amid the cold, marble statues. I went over and sat down beside him, stroking his thick dark hair. He lay back and closed his eyes, but didn't move to touch me. I studied the fine features of his face—like a statue of Apollo. If he were going to leave my life, I must memorize this face, so I'd always have it. He opened his eyes, stretched his long arms around me, and pulled me down beside him.

Like the first night we'd made love on the ship, there was a vigorous, hungry passion between us, a craving that couldn't be satiated. Light was pouring through my window when we finally stopped, exhaustion and gravity holding us down on the carpet under the table where our madness had taken us during the night.

I watched him get up and stretch. How like a sleek cat he was! He kissed me lightly on the lips, and left without a word.

33

There was no sign of him when I arrived at the office. Even his desk had been cleared out. Nicole was packing her things to leave.

"Jeanne made the right decision," said Nicole, "much as I hate to admit it. She's got to finish high school. I'm hoping she'll come out here to college. In any case, she knows she can depend on me. We'll always be friends. It was important for her to find out who her real mother was. So you and I are going to be competing," she laughed.

"This time for business." I smiled.

"There's enough in Los Angeles for the two of us."

"Men or customers?"

"Both. It's a good move for you," she said. "You'll learn a lot from Ralph. I did." She put her coffeemaker in a box and laughed. "I should take Freddy along with me to make the coffee. He's the only one I've ever known who could make decent office coffee. Well, it's a big move for me, a big change all the way around. Scott and Jeanne gone out of my life," she sighed, and looked at me. The rug burns on my back were beginning to ache. "You're still in love with him, aren't you?"

"Afraid so," I admitted.

"You'd be all wrong for him, too," she said.

"You're too much like me. He needs the sweet, sensitive kind of woman who would appreciate the scholar in him. It would drive you crazy, like it did me."

"Still, I wouldn't mind a crack at it."

"You'll have many more lovers. Exciting, wonderful affairs. Men are never in short supply for women like us." Like us? Was I already like Nicole, a brick wall around me? Was that what attracted Scott?

I helped take some boxes downstairs and load them into her car. Knowing Scott was really leaving her had made me sympathetic. I wondered that she wasn't more distraught. "Let's get together soon," I said, "for lunch. I can afford to treat you now."

We laughed, shook hands like a couple of businessmen, then on second thought, hugged like a couple of women. Nicole got into the car, started up the motor, then turned to me. "Emily, always remember what my stepmother used to say. 'You can throw 'em against the wall all day, but the only ones that count are the turds that stick.' "

34

Ralph agreed to all my plans, except the ones that were going to cost him. So I had to work it out on paper to show him where they were actually going to save him money, and increase his volume. Then he agreed.

It was noisy for a week while the cabinets were being built, the reception room door knocked out. I moved Scott's zebra couch into what was now the reception area, and was about to replace the surfer poster with the cheetah and wildebeest painting. But on a second look, I decided it would make a potential customer uneasy. I had a low counter constructed, with comfortable seats on either side. Priscilla had been canned, so there was no longer a pink mannequin to shield us from the customers.

Some minor rate changes meant we had to reprint our Hawaii brochures. I had the new ones redesigned with slick, updated photos of Waikiki. Ralph was delighted when our sales from direct mailings increased.

Al's Hundred Year War tour bombed. People were already too fed up with Vietnam and the Middle East. Vacations are purchased to get away from such ugly realities.

I was working ten and twelve hours a day, with an exuberant, creative energy I didn't know I had.

A month had gone by since I'd seen Scott, but oddly, I wasn't disturbed by it. Our last night had been Fourth of July Fireworks, a fitting end, if that's what it was, to a turbulent romance. I still wanted to see him, but the desperate longing had vanished. Had the excitement only been generated by his inaccessibility? Did I know too much about him now?

One afternoon I walked in from lunch and Scott was seated on the zebra couch. I sat down beside him.

"Doesn't look like the same place," he commented.

"Like it?"

"No. Where's your office?"

I motioned around the room. "You're a democrat," he said. "Decidedly. A woman of the people."

"Aristocrats have no place in business," I laughed. "What're you up to?"

"I'm at USC. Hell of a school. No wonder their alumni get so sickeningly dewy-eyed about the place. I'm doing my dissertation on Xenophon."

"Xeno-who? I thought that was some kind of a phobia."

"No, he was an adventurer-historian who lived around 400 BC. I had to read his stuff in beginning Greek when I was in boarding school. It was Xenophon who inspired me to run away to sea. Exciting writer. A lot of scholars have been dismissing him recently, saying he wrote historical accounts to give himself more credit, but I disagree. I'm going to prove them wrong."

"I don't mean to be rude, Scott, but what difference does it make in 1967 if he lied about what happened in 400 BC?" I saw by Scott's expression that I was irrelevant.

He produced a paperback book. "Something, eh? Still a bestseller after all these years. Look what he says when this Athenian puts down the Spartans for raising their children to steal, because as good soldiers they must learn to survive. The Spartan says:

> What I have gathered about you Athenians is that you are remarkably good at stealing public funds, even though it is a very risky business for whoever does so; and your best men are the greatest experts at it, that is if it is your best men who are considered the right people to be in government.

I looked at Scott blankly.

"Don't you see?" he asked me intently. "The world never changes. People just keep doing the same things over and over."

"That's what Cindy says."

"And it doesn't worry you at all, does it?"

"No. I'm worried about the 150 people I've got to get off to Hawaii tomorrow."

"Meet you tonight after work at the Polo Lounge." His eyes were sparkling in the old way. He smiled at me. It was the Cheshire Cat grin. "Hundred and fifty people? Xenophon had ten thousand Greek mercenary soldiers to get out of Persia."

"Ten thousand Greeks! Helen might have fought me for them, but what a fortune I could have made in charter flights!"

BESTSELLERS

☐	BEGGAR ON HORSEBACK–Thorpe	23091-0	1.50
☐	THE TURQUOISE–Seton	23088-0	1.95
☐	STRANGER AT WILDINGS–Brent	23085-6	1.95
	(Pub. in England as Kirkby's Changeling)		
☐	MAKING ENDS MEET–Howar	23084-8	1.95
☐	THE LYNMARA LEGACY–Gaskin	23060-0	1.95
☐	THE TIME OF THE DRAGON–Eden	23059-7	1.95
☐	THE GOLDEN RENDEZVOUS–MacLean	23055-4	1.75
☐	TESTAMENT–Morrell	23033-3	1.95
☐	CAN YOU WAIT TIL FRIDAY?–	23022-8	1.75
	Olson, M.D.		
☐	HARRY'S GAME–Seymour	23019-8	1.95
☐	TRADING UP–Lea	23014-7	1.95
☐	CAPTAINS AND THE KINGS–Caldwell	23069-4	2.25
☐	"I AIN'T WELL–BUT I SURE AM	23007-4	1.75
	BETTER"–Lair		
☐	THE GOLDEN PANTHER–Thorpe	23006-6	1.50
☐	IN THE BEGINNING–Potok	22980-7	1.95
☐	DRUM–Onstott	22920-3	1.95
☐	LORD OF THE FAR ISLAND–Holt	22874-6	1.95
☐	DEVIL WATER–Seton	23633-1	2.25
☐	CSARDAS–Pearson	22885-1	1.95
☐	CIRCUS–MacLean	22875-4	1.95
☐	WINNING THROUGH INTIMIDATION–	23589-0	2.25
	Ringer		
☐	THE POWER OF POSITIVE	23499-1	1.95
	THINKING–Peale		
☐	VOYAGE OF THE DAMNED–	22449-X	1.75
	Thomas & Witts		
☐	THINK AND GROW RICH–Hill	23504-1	1.95
☐	EDEN–Ellis	23543-2	1.95

Buy them at your local bookstores or use this handy coupon for ordering: